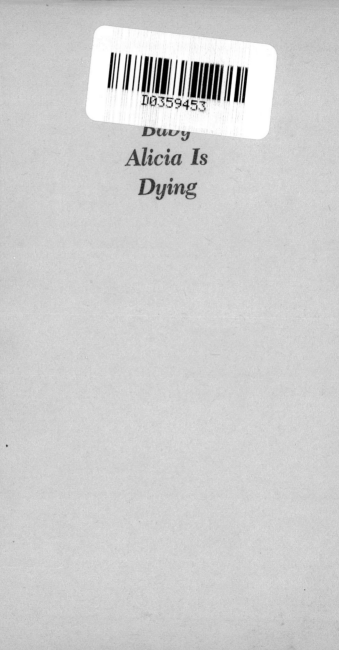

Baby
Alicia Is
Dying

Baby Alicia Is Dying

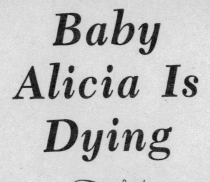

Lurlene McDaniel

BANTAM BOOKS
NEW YORK · TORONTO · LONDON · SYDNEY · AUCKLAND

RL 5, age 10 and up

BABY ALICIA IS DYING
A Bantam Book / June 1993

*The Starfire logo is a registered trademark of Bantam Books,
a division of Bantam Doubleday Dell Publishing Group, Inc.
Registered in U.S. Patent and Trademark Office and elsewhere.*

ISBN 0-553-29605-1

Published simultaneously in the United States and Canada

---

*Bantam Books are published by Bantam Books, a division of Bantam
Doubleday Dell Publishing Group, Inc. Its trademark, consisting of the
words "Bantam Books" and the portrayal of a rooster, is Registered in
U.S. Patent and Trademark Office and in other countries. Marca Regis-
trada. Bantam Books, 1540 Broadway, New York, New York 10036.*

PRINTED IN THE UNITED STATES OF AMERICA

RAD   10 9 8 7 6 5 4 3 2

I would like to thank the staff and volunteers of Childkind, Atlanta, Georgia; Kim Hankins for her expertise; and Sandy Wilson Sommers, a friend.

"Then the righteous will answer him, 'Lord, when did we see you hungry and feed you, or thirsty and give you something to drink? When did we see you a stranger and invite you in, or needing clothes and clothe you? When did we see you sick or in prison and go to visit you?'
"The King will reply, 'I tell you the truth, whatever you did for one of the least of these brothers of mine, you did for me.' "

MATTHEW 25:37–40

Chapter One

~——~

"You're lucky, Val. I wish I was old enough to live away at college," Desila Mitchell said with a sigh as she watched her older sister packing.

"Cheer up, Desi. This will be you in four more years. Then again, you're so smart, it may take only three."

Desi grimaced. She knew she had brains, but she felt ordinary and lacked her sister's self-confidence. "Besides," Val added, "I thought you were excited about being a freshman at Grady. Ninth grade will be fun."

Desi hooked her arm around the post of her sister's antique bed and shrugged. "It's just that Grady's so different and so big. I'll bet half of Atlanta goes there."

"Just the 'cool' half," Val joked as she heaped sweaters into a steamer trunk. "Believe me, good old Grady isn't so bad once you learn your way around."

Desi knew it was easy for Val to shrug off her misgivings. Val had been especially popular during her four years at Grady High. "When will you come home again?" Desi asked.

"I have four days over Thanksgiving. Two weeks at Christmas."

"But that's months from now."

"Just three. The University of Florida is only a day's drive, you know. It's not like I'll be on another planet. You can write, and I might even answer," Val said with a wink as she rummaged through her bureau drawer. "Have you seen my navy blue cardigan?"

"If you hadn't landed that tennis scholarship, you would be starting at the community college and living at home."

"If I weren't on tennis scholarship, I doubt I'd be going to college at all, even though Mom and Dad wanted me to. You know I'm no scholar." Val slammed one drawer and tore through another as she talked. "Mom!" she yelled. "Mom, can you come help me?" Val walked around Desi, saying, "You should find something fun to do. You know, Grady has lots of after-school stuff—"

"Forget it. I'm no good at sports, and I've never been a club person. The most I'll do is my annual science fair project." Desi had been entering science fairs ever since her first collection of insects had earned her a blue ribbon in third grade. She'd never been afraid of bugs or spiders; in fact she'd always felt more comfortable with four-legged creatures than with two-legged dolls. "Do you know what Corrine told me they're doing for biology elective at Grady this year?"

"What?"

"They're making one big class by putting the smartest of us ninth graders in with the sophomores who flunked biology last year and have to repeat the course."

"So what?"

"I love biology. I don't want to be in with a bunch of rejects."

"Sounds to me like you might get to help out some poor soul who couldn't cut it," Val replied sympathetically.

"I get to look forward to a symbiotic relationship with sophomore fungi!"

Val rolled her eyes, picked up her tennis racquet, plucked at the webbing as if it were a guitar, and sang, "Maybe you'll find 'love.' "

Desi burst out laughing. She was really going to miss her older sister.

"Did you want something, honey?" their mother asked as she came into the room, breathless from climbing the stairs.

"I can't find my navy blue cardigan anywhere."

"It's at the cleaner's."

"But we're leaving for Florida in two days!"

"I plan to pick it up tomorrow." Their mother turned to Desi. "Please don't hang on the bedpost. You'll work it loose."

Desi dropped her hands quickly. "Sorry."

"Shouldn't you be getting your clothes together for the start of school too?"

"I've got until Monday before classes begin. No rush."

"Yes, but your father and I plan to stay in Gainesville during the week of freshman orientation, and you'll be staying with Aunt Clare." Mom touched the black cascade of Valerie's hair, and Desi felt a twinge of envy. Their mother never seemed to touch her with the affection she showed Val. "Don't you want to stay with her?"

"Sure I do! It's just that it's my first week of high school."

"Well, it's Val's first week of college."

And Valerie's more important than I am, Desi thought. Hadn't it always been that way? Val first, Desi second. Pride over Val's tennis accomplishments and nothing for Desi's science achievements. Val's beauty over Desi's plainness.

"I *can* make it through orientation alone," Val offered good-naturedly. "I *am* a big girl now."

"We've had these plans for months," Mom said. "Your father's got another dentist covering his patients, and I don't start working full-time until after Labor Day. No need to juggle the schedule. Aunt Clare can handle Desi's needs for a week."

"I give up!" Val announced in exasperation. "Deciding what to take and what to leave is impossible."

"Let me help," Mom said. "It's simply a matter of organizing things."

Desi started to offer her help too, but her

mother and Valerie weren't paying any attention to her. *They don't need you,* she told herself. After a few moments she slipped quietly from the room, realizing that they didn't even notice she'd gone.

"I've rented some movies for the weekend. Pick out one to watch while I go change. I'm so tired! Would you toss a bag of popcorn into the microwave?" Aunt Clare asked as she thrust open the door of her spacious town house. Desi lugged her suitcase inside.

"Let me stick my bag in my room first." Desi headed to the room that was as familiar as her own bedroom. She shoved her suitcase into the closet, kicked off her sneakers, then went to the kitchen and found the popcorn.

Aunt Clare breezed into the kitchen minutes later. "I guess Valerie and your folks got off all right."

"The minivan was jam-packed. Mom was making Dad and Val crazy, but they hit the road about ten this morning."

Aunt Clare offered an understanding smile. "I know how Eva can be. She used to drive me crazy when we were growing up because she was such a perfectionist. But when you begin life as the prettiest girl in Athens, Georgia, become homecoming queen and tennis star extraordinaire, then marry the cutest guy in the class—well, I guess it's hard to contend with us common people."

Desi felt that Aunt Clare was the only person in the world who understood her mother the way *she* did. "I'm not hitting on your mom, you understand," her aunt added hastily. "But life has been generous with her. She grew up being treated like a princess and has had only one tragedy in all of her years on earth."

"You mean when the baby died?" Desi felt more curious than remorseful about the incident. After all, it had happened before she was even born. Val had been two when the baby, a boy, had died at three months.

"I honestly didn't think Eva was going to make it. There's nothing sadder than sudden infant death syndrome." Aunt Clare put bowls, napkins, and glasses onto bamboo lap trays while she spoke. "Fortunately, in all my years of nursing, I've only had to deal with two other cases. Parents put a perfectly normal baby down to sleep and hours later come back to find their baby is dead. SIDS is a terrible thing."

Desi tried to imagine what it must have been like for her family. No one ever talked about the loss. It was as if the baby had never existed. "All I've ever heard is that Mom had a tough time. I wish I knew more about it," Desi confided.

Aunt Clare stared off into space, her mouth set in a grim line. "There's not much to know. Your mother finally came out of it. After she had you, she took that interior decorating course, and her life seemed to get back on track. And then of course, with Val being so gifted in tennis—much as Eva had been—well, that gave her life new direction as well."

Desi wanted to tell her aunt that to her way of thinking, "having her" had been a mistake. Her mother would have been far better off devoting herself to her part-time decorating job and managing Val's tennis circuit. "Once Mom starts her job full-time," Desi observed, "she'll probably be even busier than she is now."

"I know. I almost wish she wouldn't."

"Why?" Desi set the timer on the microwave. "You work full-time."

"She still has *you* at home. She needs to give you the same amount of attention she's given Valerie. That's my opinion," she said, flashing Desi a smile.

Even though Desi had often wished the same thing, she didn't want her aunt criticizing her mother. "It's no big deal, Aunt Clare. Val says I'll be so busy with high school, I won't even notice Mom and Dad are around."

The timer went off, Aunt Clare removed and opened the bag, and the rich, buttery aroma of popped corn filled the kitchen. "I work because I don't have a family and because I love nursing," her aunt declared.

Aunt Clare had never married. Her fiancé, a medical resident, had been killed in a car accident, and she never allowed herself to fall in love again.

"I can't wait until I have a career," Desi said. "I'll make money to spend on the things I want. After college, of course."

Aunt Clare filled bowls with popcorn and handed a tray to Desi. "I'm not exactly on the Fortune 500 list, dear. Come on. Let's go sit on the sofa and watch some movies."

"Well, you're not poor either," Desi replied as she dropped to the couch.

"There are trade-offs."

"Like what?"

Her aunt set her tray onto the glass-topped coffee table and snuggled into the corner of the sofa, facing Desi. "You're the only 'daughter' I'll ever have."

Desi smiled, pleased. It was no secret that she was her aunt's favorite niece. That often helped her feel better about not being her mother's favorite daughter. "You might still get married and have kids."

"No way. I'm married to the hospital," Aunt Clare said with a laugh. "That's quite enough for me."

"Mom told me you've changed positions at the hospital."

"I sure have."

"Are you going to tell me about it?"

Aunt Clare tipped her head thoughtfully. "Actually, I'd rather show you."

"You make it sound mysterious."

"Not at all. My job has expanded, that's all. I'm doing my usual administrative duties with the pediatric nursing staff, and I've just been appointed community liaison between County Hospital and Atlanta's ChildCare house."

"I've never heard of ChildCare."

Aunt Clare smiled as she said, "I have a great idea. Since you'll be staying here this week, why don't you come with me next Saturday and see ChildCare for yourself? I think you'll be very interested."

Chapter Two

"Desi! Over here!"

Desi searched the crowded hallway for the voice calling her name. She flattened herself against a bank of lockers in an attempt to get out of the crush.

"Desi! I'm coming!"

She saw Corrine Johnson, her best friend since fifth grade, struggling to pass through the mass of milling students. Desi reached out and caught Corrine's hand and pulled her the rest of the way toward her. "Do I still have all my body parts?" Corrine asked breathlessly. "This place is a madhouse! I'm totally lost."

"Me too," Desi confessed, staring down at the map of Grady that had come in her freshman packet.

"Show me your class schedule card."

Desi fumbled with her notebook and extracted her card. "I've got biology first period." She had to shout to be heard over the noise. "I think the room's upstairs."

"I've got English." Corrine handed her card back. "All we have together is lunch. That stinks. I'm hoping we'll have some really cute guys in class."

"Corrine, this is the big time. No Grady High guys are going be interested in freshmen peasants like us. Besides, I've got to concentrate on my grades if I hope to get a scholarship to college and medical school."

The bell rang. "Here we go," Corrine declared.

"Look for me in the cafeteria," Desi called. "If we miss each other, call me tonight." Desi watched her friend weave through the mass of bodies and felt a wave of nostalgia. She and Corrine were different in many ways, but she still wanted them to be friends, and she hoped that different schedules in high school didn't drive them apart.

Desi wedged herself into the flow of the crowd. She allowed herself to be carried along toward the stairs, hoping desperately that her class was indeed on the upper level. She found the correct door and entered, as a paper airplane sailed in front of her nose. She ducked and took a seat in an already crowded room. The room was arranged with lab tables where groups of four could work at the same time. Shiny stainless sinks, glass beakers, and test tubes formed the center of each lab table. Posters of animals and plants lined one wall.

The teacher, Mr. Redding, arrived as the tardy bell sounded. He took attendance and assigned lab partners. Since there was an uneven number of kids, Desi found herself in a threesome. She was grouped with a girl, Shaundra Johnson, and a boy, Brian Connley. Desi thought that Shaundra wore too much eye makeup and that Brian didn't look like a "serious" student. His shock of blond hair hung low over his forehead, almost obscuring his intense blue eyes. He was big and muscular and wore a rawhide band around his wrist. She felt intimidaded by his size.

They listened as Mr. Redding outlined the course work. After he passed out worksheets, he allowed the students to discuss the material among themselves. "Man, I hate this stuff," Shaundra complained as she shoved the paper aside.

"Me too," Brian agreed.

"I think it could be fun," Desi ventured.

Shaundra gave her a bored stare. "I flunked this course cold last year, and I don't have any hopes of doing much better this year."

"I failed it too," Brian admitted with a shrug. "Actually, I might have passed it, but I guess I cut too many classes."

Desi realized she was the lone freshman in the group, and the only one interested in biology. "It says here that we'll be dissecting earthworms and frogs during this grading period."

"Count me out!" Shaundra declared. "That stuff's disgusting!"

Brian plopped his head dramatically against the tabletop. "Now I remember why I skipped so many classes."

"I don't mind that part," she told them. "I like science."

"You're weird," Shaundra said, making Desi blush bright red.

"We have to keep a journal," Brian said, and just as Desi wondered if she was going to be responsible for that too, he added, "I can do that part. It's just keeping accurate track of our experiments. I know from last year how Redding wants it done." Desi was skeptical of his offer, but she wrote his name down next to the assignment in her notebook. Obviously Mr. Redding expected his class to perform in tandem. She wanted to ask Shaundra what she was going to contribute to the group, but didn't have the nerve.

"If we want extra credit, we can do a special project," Desi announced as she scanned the course outline. "We might want to consider one, you know. If it gets into the science fair finals, it will be a guaranteed A in this class." She looked from Brian to Shaundra, but they seemed indifferent.

Brian explained, "Look, I'm not planning to knock myself out for this class. I just want to *pass.*"

Desi was disappointed. This was a class she was most interested in. She'd hoped for more cooperation from her partners. Briefly she toyed with asking Mr. Redding to give her other lab partners, but decided to wait and give Shaundra and Brian a chance. Finally the bell rang, and everyone darted for the door.

Desi missed Corrine at lunch, and by the time she'd finished the day and caught the city bus for her aunt's town house, she felt as if she'd been dragged by a rope behind dirt bikes.

That evening her parents called. "How was your first day?" her father asked.

"Hectic." She didn't add that she missed them and wished they all could have been together. "But I like biology, and I think I'll do all right in it if my lab partners cooperate."

Her dad chuckled. "That's my girl! Val wants to talk to you."

"The campus here is awesome," Val told her when she got on the phone. "There's ivy on the bricks of all these really old buildings. Tennis starts tomorrow, and it's going to be a killer. So far I'm coming in top-seeded among all the freshmen girls."

"That's good." Desi felt proud of her sister, but realized that once again Valerie would be the family star.

"It's sort of scary," Val admitted. "People keep expecting great things from me. I hope I don't let them down."

Desi doubted it would be a problem and told Valerie as much.

"Here's Mom," Val said.

Desi's mother got on and announced, "Val's already very respected in the athletic department." Desi could practically see her beaming smile through the receiver. "Are things going well with you and Aunt Clare? Was school all right?"

"School's fine, and Aunt Clare and I are having a great time. She's taking me someplace Saturday. It's connected with her new job."

"Well, don't get in her way," her mother instructed, and then asked to speak to her sister.

"I won't, Mom." She handed over the phone and stood aside, wishing that her mother had talked to her longer. It seemed to Desi that her mother was always busy and rushed whenever it came to her. Her mom had time for Val, but never quite enough time for her. It had been that way for as long as she could remember, but she doubted it would change now. *Learn to live with it,* she told herself, and quietly left the room.

The Saturday morning air was crystal clear. Aunt Clare's car wove its way down a quiet suburban street and turned into a driveway situated between two low brick walls. A small plaque posted on one wall read: *ChildCare.* The driveway curved gracefully toward twin magnolia trees standing on a hilly crest. Behind them a brick, ranch-style house stretched across a tree-cluttered lawn in need of cutting.

Aunt Clare parked beside a back door, saying, "Let's go in through the kitchen. I want to introduce you to some people before the meeting begins."

Inside, two women were rushing around frantically, trying to quiet and feed five screaming infants.

Desi saw three high chairs, a playpen, and an infant seat scattered about. One of the women looked up. "Clare! Thank heavens you're here." As she handed Desi's aunt a bowl of baby food and a spoon, she said, "I'll bet this is your niece."

Desi opened her mouth to speak, but the woman held up her hand. "Formal introductions later. I'm Gayle. This is Anthony." She handed the screaming boy over to Clare, scooped up the baby wailing in the playpen, and turned to Desi. "I've got Dwayne. Can you please give this bottle to Alicia there?" She pointed to the baby crying in the infant seat.

"But I've never—"

"Just put it between her lips. She'll take it from there," Gayle urged good-naturedly as she shoveled glop into Dwayne's opening mouth. "Five-month-old tots aren't noted for their patience."

Gingerly Desi scooped Alicia from the infant seat, trying not to drop the bottle. She sat in a nearby rocker and rested the baby's head in the crook of her arm, and pushed the nipple of the bottle against Alicia's mouth. Instantly the baby began sucking greedily. Blessed quiet descended on the room.

The little girl's eyes were large and dark brown and fringed with incredibly long lashes. Tiny teardrops clung to the lashes' tips. Narrow tracks of moisture had stained her dark-skinned cheeks. Alicia's hair was a mass of black fuzz, and against Desi's bare arm it felt soft, like feathers.

Once the edge was off Alicia's appetite, the baby slowed her sucking and stared intently upward. Her open, curious expression made Desi smile. "Hi. Are you full yet?" Desi felt a surge of pleasure as she watched the infant in her arms.

Alicia reached, and Desi held her finger up. Alicia's small hand wrapped around it. The baby's perfect, miniature fingers were no bigger than a doll's. Desi smiled broadly, and the baby spit the nipple out. Formula dribbled down her chin, but slowly her face broke into a matching smile. The beauty of it took Desi's breath away.

Gayle chuckled and said, "You better watch out for that one, honey. She's a real heartbreaker."

Dimples peeked from either side of Alicia's bow-shaped mouth, and her eyes resembled soft, shimmering pools of dancing brown light. "You're so beautiful," Desi said, surprised by the infant's effect on her.

"Hard to believe no one wants her," Aunt Clare said from over Desi's shoulder.

"She's an orphan?"

"Not exactly. Her mother abandoned her at birth."

Desi couldn't believe it. "Why? How can a mother not want her own baby?"

"Because Alicia"—she gestured toward the

others—"as well as these other babies were born testing HIV-positive."

Incredulous, Desi glanced from baby to baby. "All of them?"

"Sad, but true. They all carry the AIDS virus."

Chapter Three

❦

"They've got AIDS?" Desi had heard much about acquired immune deficiency syndrome over the past year. A few highly publicized cases of some important, well-known people had prompted awareness programs at her former school. She knew the virus was passed through an exchange of body fluids —like blood or semen. "But how did they get it?" Desi asked.

"Their mothers are intravenous drug users," Gayle explained, coming over, balancing a hefty and satisfied baby Dwayne on her hip. "They shared needles, and the virus passed to the fetuses before they were born. Dwayne here is almost a year old. He was born HIV-positive *and* addicted to cocaine." The baby flashed a toothless grin that lit up his dark face.

"But they *look* healthy," Desi declared.

"They are healthy right now. But we're finding that many HIV-positive infants develop full-blown AIDS before they're a year old." Dwayne started squealing, so Gayle set him down in the playpen and handed him a toy. "Researchers are also discovering that once the baby develops an immune system of its own, the baby *sometimes* stops testing positive."

"Will Alicia get AIDS?" Desi asked. Already she felt a soft spot growing inside her heart for the little girl. The baby was so cute, and she kept watching Desi with avid interest.

"The jury's still out," Gayle replied. "We just have to wait and see."

"But AIDS is fatal," Desi said, remembering that AIDS destroys a person's immune system, making it impossible to fight off infections.

"True, but new therapies are helping victims live longer. However, even without developing AIDS, these babies are very susceptible to bacteria and viruses." Gayle dabbed Alicia's chin with a clean tissue. The baby held more tightly to Desi. "With these babies it's usually pneumonia or infections of the esophagus, which means they can't eat or drink. Then they get dehydrated. Anthony over there's been back to the hospital twice already, and he's just ten months old."

At the sound of his name Anthony slapped his hand on the tray of his high chair. "But you said that some of them do get better—they never get AIDS."

"These days, we know more about the disease, and our treatments are better. Infants born with low T cell counts and symptoms of HIV can benefit from drugs like AZT. Some babies are even transfused, given immunogammaglobulin—IMg therapy —to build up their resistance."

Desi's head was swimming with all the information and the unfamiliar medical terms when a woman entered the kitchen and announced, "Gayle, you've got people waiting out in the playroom. What should I tell them?"

"The meeting!" Gayle slapped herself on the forehead. "Thanks, Sadie." She motioned to Clare and Desi. "Come on out and meet the volunteers who are going to help us with the babies here at ChildCare."

"Volunteers?" Desi felt interested.

"That's what my new job is all about," Aunt Clare explained. "Most HIV-positive babies are born at County Hospital. It's my job to coordinate hospital efforts to give these babies a more suitable environment, when they're medically stable, with ChildCare's interest in providing a home for them. Follow me. You'll understand better once you listen to Gayle."

"You want me to take Alicia?" Sadie asked. The infant had fallen asleep in Desi's arms.

Desi cuddled her tenderly. "That's all right. No use waking her up." Nestling the sleeping baby, Desi followed Gayle and Aunt Clare through the length of the house into a blue-carpeted room filled with playpens and baby toys. About twenty men and women were seated on sofas, chairs, and the floor. Desi and her aunt settled between two well-dressed women on a well-worn sofa. Gayle began to speak.

"I'm overwhelmed by the turnout—thank you.

I'm Gayle Sommers, volunteer coordinator for ChildCare. We desperately need your help with the care and nurturing of our ChildCare children. Until this home opened last year, some HIV-positive babies never left County Hospital—living all their lives in a cheerless ward because there was no place for them to go. We know that the hospital staff do the best they can, but they have many patients to care for and can't give these babies the undivided attention they need.

"Some babies have been placed in foster homes around the Atlanta area; five others are living here. This house, the two acres of property, the furnishings—everything has been donated by concerned citizens, local churches, and health care professionals to give HIV-positive children a place to grow up and to be loved."

Gayle paced the room, weaving among the listeners as she spoke. "We have two full-time foster parents here on staff. They live upstairs and are the primary caregivers of the babies. But as you know, babies are a *lot* of work every minute of the day."

Voices in the room murmured in agreement. "That's why we need volunteers. Naturally these little ones must be fed, bathed, and changed, but they need emotional nourishment as much as they need the physical. Developmentally they're behind other infants their age. They're slower to gain weight, crawl, feed themselves—most normal activities.

"We can improve their lot in life by providing

family bonding. They need to see the same faces on a consistent basis. They need to be held and played with and loved. In other words they need you."

Desi gazed down at the sleeping Alicia. The baby looked so small and cuddly in her sleeper. Her long eyelashes almost brushed her cheeks, and her rosebud mouth was puckered above her dainty, pointed chin. *How could a mother* not *love her?* Desi wondered. Then she remembered her own mother's preference for Valerie.

"That's why we ask you to volunteer here at ChildCare only if you can stick with the program," Gayle continued, forcing Desi to gather her wandering thoughts. "Consistency is the key. Of course we understand that sometimes circumstances come up, but by and large, if you volunteer for a specific time to be here, it's important that you show up. The babies will come to know your faces and your touches. They'll come to depend on you like parents."

"What if one of the babies gets sick?" a woman asked.

"Sick babies go back to the hospital, and when they get well, they come back here, to their home."

"But since they're HIV-positive," another woman asked, "won't they require special handling?"

"Every volunteer must go through our orientation program. You'll learn CPR and basic first aid. You'll learn how to properly dispose of soiled diapers

—the health department does a special pickup twice a week. You'll be taught how to make formula, sterilize bottles, prepare food. We'll teach you all you need to know."

"How about the risk of getting AIDS from them?" a man asked. *Don't these people know anything?* Desi wondered. She knew a person couldn't catch AIDS through casual contact.

"Studies of kids already placed in foster homes show that such activities as hugging and kissing—even the sharing of toothbrushes—do not spread the virus," Gayle told him. "Actually it's far more likely that these babies can catch something from us. That's why we ask you not to come if you have a cold or a sore throat. You could infect one of them, and because their immune systems are weakened, the baby could get very sick."

Alicia stirred in Desi's arms and stretched. Desi lifted the infant to her shoulder, and Alicia's head flopped into the crook of her neck. Then the baby promptly fell back asleep.

"So their mothers have given them up?" a woman asked.

"Not in every case," Gayle explained. "Some of the mothers signed them away immediately after giving birth and learning about their HIV-positive status. Others haven't given up custody and may reclaim their babies if they prove they can be responsible for them."

Desi didn't think any mother deserved to have

her baby returned if she had deliberately rejected it. Gayle said, "If a mother wants her child again, the human resources department sets up supervised visits and evaluates the mother's competence. If she proves she can handle the responsibility of caring for and raising her child, she can have custody."

"So what should we do if we want to volunteer our help?" someone asked.

"I'll pass around a sign-up sheet with the hours we need covered. Feel free to come more than once a week. I'll contact each of you soon to set up a day for group training."

"I want to be a volunteer," Desi whispered to her aunt as the paper went around the room. Something had stirred inside her toward these helpless and, for the most part, unwanted babies. They were children in need of love and attention. Desi realized she had a lot of both to give.

"Are you sure? The work is time-consuming."

"There's nothing at school I'm really interested in doing. And with Valerie at college and mom starting work full-time, I think it's something I'd like doing. The babies are cute, and no one wants them. I think that's awful."

"Shouldn't you check with your parents first?"

With Valerie gone, Desi doubted her parents would be interested in her activities at all. "I'm sure it'll be all right. If I can figure out a way of getting here."

"I can make arrangements to pick you up from

school and drop you off. I know how much Child-Care could use the help."

Desi lowered the sleeping Alicia from her shoulder and gazed at her adorable features. It wasn't fair that this baby should be so small and helpless and have so much stacked against her. Her life had just started. She looked from Alicia to her aunt. "I'd like to help out. I really would."

Chapter Four

"A volunteer taking care of AIDS babies! You can't be serious," her mother declared when Desi told her parents what she wanted to do.

They had returned from Gainesville late the night before, and now everyone was seated at the dining room table in Clare's town house having Sunday dinner. Aunt Clare had set the table elegantly—as if for a special occasion—with her fine French imported lace tablecloth, her best bone china, and silver candlesticks. "Why would you want to do such a thing?"

"Because I just want to," Desi replied stubbornly. "Besides, none of the babies have AIDS. They're only HIV-positive."

"AIDS is a terrible disease," her mother countered. "There's plenty medical science doesn't know about it. What if you somehow become infected?"

"I work with AIDS patients at the hospital, Eva," Clare said. "We take precautions."

"You're an adult, and what you do as part of your health care training is your business. But Desi's just a child. Why should she needlessly put herself at risk?"

"Eva, think rationally," Aunt Clare replied. "No one's 'at risk' helping out at ChildCare."

"Don't patronize me, Clare. I read the papers and watch TV. I understand plenty about HIV and AIDS."

Desi bit her tongue to keep from screaming. She was fourteen—hardly a child—and her mother was totally ignoring the fact that working at Child-Care was something she wanted to do. "I'll be okay," she blurted. "If you could just see these little babies—"

"Bill, tell these two lunatics that this venture is out of the question," her mother interrupted, and turned toward Desi's father. He had shoved his chair backward and was listening, but hadn't made a comment yet.

"I frequently handle AIDS patients in my practice, Eva. My hygienist and I are extremely careful. We double-glove and wear masks. I see no reason to deny someone proper dental care."

"But you're a professional. Desi isn't."

He looked at Desi. "School's important. I wouldn't want your grades to fall."

"My studies will come first. I have no intention of blowing it academically."

"Look, I can't understand why a girl with all your advantages would want to put yourself out for a group of strangers' babies," Desi's mother said. "Surely a school the size of Grady can offer you things to do—sports, clubs, music. This is high school, Desi. You should be having fun."

"Mom, I've never been into clubs. That's Val's thing. I'm *me*. I *really* want to do work at ChildCare. Please don't say no." Bright sunlight poured through the bay window of Aunt Clare's dining room, throwing light across her mother's long dark hair and fine-boned features. Desi couldn't help thinking that her mother was still quite beautiful. What a disappointment Desi felt she must be to her. Desi was so unlike her mother. So unlike Valerie.

For a moment silence descended on the room, and all Desi could hear was the sound of her own breathing. Her father finally spoke. "I have no objection to Desi's performing community service, Eva. I know Clare will keep an eye on her."

"Of course I will."

Her mother glared at each of them, and gripped the arms of the graceful Queen Anne dining chair until her knuckles went white. "Well, it certainly appears that I'm outnumbered, doesn't it? I'm not in favor of this, Desi. I know you think I'm being overly harsh and unsympathetic, but I don't care. I have my reasons."

"And I have mine," Desi insisted. This was something she wanted because it would be *hers*. She wouldn't be following in Val's or even her mother's high school footsteps. Her mom and Val could be pretty, athletic, and popular. She wanted to be useful and valuable.

"I start work full-time next week. I won't be able to shuttle you to and from this ChildCare house," her mother warned.

"I'll be responsible for driving Desi," Aunt Clare interjected.

"I won't bother you about it, Mom."

Still agitated, Desi's mother rose and started clearing her place.

"Don't do that, Eva," Aunt Clare said cheerily. "You're my guests today. I'll do it."

"It's all right, Clare. You've done quite enough for us today already. Quite enough."

Juggling plates and glassware, Desi's mother left the room in a huff.

Because Corrine was out of town over the weekend, Desi was unable to talk to her until Monday at lunch about ChildCare.

"So tell me," Corrine said after listening to Desi describe the volunteer program, "are there any cute guy volunteers?"

"Get serious, Corrine. This isn't about meeting guys, it's about helping abandoned babies."

"It doesn't sound like much fun to me." Corrine poked her fork into a mound of mashed potatoes and watched the gravy leak onto her plate.

"The babies are so adorable. Like little dolls. Alicia, the one who fell asleep in my arms, is the cutest thing I've ever seen." Talking about Alicia made Desi smile tenderly.

"Kittens and puppies are cute. Babies just spit up and poop. I *know*, I baby-sit all the time. You've never had to make money baby-sitting, Desi. You'll see—it'll get old fast, believe me." Corrine took a sip from the straw in her milk carton. "Besides, what do you know about babies? You've cared more about bugs and butterflies for years! Why this sudden interest in babies?"

For a moment Desi wasn't sure what to say. Corrine was right—she'd never baby-sat because her mother had always discouraged both her and Valerie from baby-sitting. "Too much responsibility," she had told them. "What if you had an emergency with someone else's child? Or an accident? It would ruin your life. If you need money, we'll up your allowance."

"First of all, I think the babies are cute," Desi replied between mouthfuls of potato chips. "And second of all, these babies need love. They've never had mothers to take care of them. I want to help. You should come and see for yourself. I'm sure they could use more volunteers."

"No way. I have big plans for myself in high school." Corrine's fork clattered against her plate. "When do you start?"

"I have an all-day training class next Saturday, then it's two afternoons a week. Some Saturdays too."

"We won't get to do much together on Saturdays if you're busy volunteering every weekend!"

"Not every Saturday. I'll have to see how many volunteers there are and when I'm most needed."

"Do you have to do this, Desi?" Corrine's green eyes looked troubled. "We've been friends *forever*, and I just thought this year was going to be extra special."

"You sound like my mother. Try to understand. It's not that I don't want to do things with you. It's just that ChildCare and these babies need me. School isn't enough for me. I want to do something meaningful with my time."

"Friday night's the first football game of the year. Are you still coming with me?" Corrine abandoned the topic.

"Sure," Desi told her with more enthusiasm than she felt. "I'm not letting this new project take over my life completely."

"I think you're wasting your time." Corrine mumbled. "There's lots to do around Grady—with me."

"It's my time," Desi said stubbornly. "It's my life."

That Friday night Corrine's dad dropped them off at the football stadium. Desi wore a new red sweater that perked up her brown hair and green eyes. By halftime the Grady High Warriors were ahead by a touchdown and she had yelled herself hoarse. "I could sure use a soda," she shouted above the noise of the marching band.

Corrine yelled, "The line's a mile long. We'd better go now if we want don't want to miss the kickoff."

They were returning from the refreshment stand when Desi saw Brian Connley walking with a group of his friends. "Hey, Desi. How're you doing?"

She was surprised that he spoke to her, since he barely acknowledged her in class. "Fine." She racked her brain for something witty to say and wished she were more like Valerie, who had a gift for small talk. "Good game, huh?"

He tossed his unruly thatch of blond hair off his forehead. "If you like football," he said with a grin. "I just came to pick up pretty girls. What are you doing after the game?"

It took Desi a moment to realize he'd paid her a compliment. She felt a warm blush creep up her neck, but thought of no snappy comeback.

"Aw, Connley, back off," one of Brian's friends said. "Can't you see the chick is elsewhere?"

"She just needs a little prodding." Brian put his arm around her shoulders, and she felt dwarfed beside him.

"More like hog-tying," one of the guys said, making the others laugh.

More color flooded Desi's cheeks. "The game's starting. I'd better go."

"See you in lab," Brian called as she turned, grabbed Corrine's arm, and bolted for the bleachers.

"Who was that?" Corrine asked. "He's gorgeous —what a build. Why'd you run off?"

"Brian was just joking. He's only my lab partner in biology."

"Well, thanks for sharing."

"I hardly know him. He was showing off for his friends, all right?"

"You're beginning to act weird, and the year's just begun, Desila Mitchell." Desi hated it when Corrine used her full name, because it meant she was ticked off. "I don't understand what's happening to you."

"Nothing's happening. Let's just watch the game, okay? Anyway I've got to get home early. Remember, I've got that class tomorrow, and my aunt's picking me up at eight o'clock."

"Right. The AIDS babies and your important new work." Corrine turned her attention to the action on the football field, but Desi had the distinct impression that her friend was politely tuning her out. Desi shivered, and felt certain that her chill had come from more than the autumn air.

Chapter Five

❧

Desi was barely in the door of the ChildCare house on her first afternoon of volunteer work when a girl she'd not yet met called, "Welcome to the zoo! Come quick! I could use a hand."

"What do you need?" Desi stepped over the toy-littered kitchen floor. Dwayne and Anthony were bopping each other with plastic blocks and yowling, Alicia was crying inside a playpen, and the girl was holding another squalling baby.

"Separate those two," the girl said. "And pick up poor Alicia—she's having a hissy fit. I've got to change this one's smelly diaper."

Desi plopped Dwayne in the playpen and patted him gently. Then she scooped up Alicia, who stopped crying as soon as Desi held her. Desi juggled Alicia and knelt down next to the girl who was busy changing the fourth baby's diaper on a changing mat she'd spread on the floor.

"Hi. I'm Tamara Wilcox," the girl said with a bright smile. "Sadie's bathing Paul, and Mrs. Randall —that's the housemother—is upstairs on the phone. I was doing fine until Heather here decided to drop a load. You must be Desi. Glad to meet you."

Desi thought that Tamara talked faster than anybody she'd ever heard. "Glad to meet you too."

"Listen, you'd better check Alicia's diaper. She just got up from her nap, and I haven't had time to change her yet."

Desi lay Alicia down carefully and fished a paper diaper out of a nearby box. The baby's lower lip began to tremble. "Now don't cry," Desi cooed. "I'm just putting dry seat covers on you. It won't hurt one little bit." Alicia seemed to study her with huge, soulful eyes.

Tamara resnapped Heather's terrycloth sleeper. Desi watched her fingers fly over the task effortlessly. Her own fingers felt clumsy and awkward as she fumbled with the tape tabs on the paper diaper. "Have you been doing this long?" she asked.

"I started over the summer," Tamara said, sitting Heather upright. "I had to cut back my hours when school started again, but I love it here."

"You sure seem to know what you're doing."

"I should—I've got three sisters and two brothers. I'm the oldest. I've always helped my mom with the others. I just *love* babies anyway."

"Do you go to Grady?"

"Goodness no!" Tamara said, her dark eyes growing large. "My daddy's a minister, and we have a school connected with our church—I'm a sophomore. My daddy thinks Grady High School is too big and impersonal." She paused and giggled self-consciously. "Whoops! I'll bet you go there." Desi nodded. "Sorry about that," Tamara said. "Didn't mean to knock it. Daddy says I always speak before I think."

"Don't worry about it. I've been there for a month already, and I still get lost going to the bathroom."

Tamara laughed. "I'm glad you're a volunteer. Most of the women who help out are older. You know—nice, but boring." She clamped her hand over her mouth. "There I go again. A lot of them go to our church, and now I've probably made you think the wrong thing."

"It's all right—I know what you're saying. Is volunteering here some sort of project for your church?"

"Yes. Daddy's big on caring for our fellowman and all. He says that's it's not enough to talk about doing good, we need to take action." Tamara thumped her open palm with her fist in what Desi surmised was an imitation of her father. "Daddy says that Jesus didn't just preach to people, but he also fed and healed them, and that's what we should do too. Our church took ChildCare on as a project last year, and it's my favorite one."

By now Heather was attempting to crawl under a chair, and Anthony banged a pot and pan gleefully. "Goodness!" Tamara exclaimed, taking Dwayne over to the others. "Looks like Alicia's the only tame baby here today. She must like you, Desi. Look how hard she's staring at you."

The infant gazed intently at Desi, who smiled down at her and said, "You're such a sweet little girl." Alicia offered one of her sunny smiles. "I can't believe her mother doesn't want her. She's so darling."

"Me either, but I'm glad there's a place like this for her. We have people in our church who do volunteer work in the projects. They talk about how drugs and gangs are everywhere. That's no place for a baby to grow up."

Desi agreed, hating to imagine baby Alicia in such an environment. "Come on. We'd better take these guys out into the playroom," Tamara said. "Anthony loves the baby swing. Let's put him in it." She picked up Heather and darted after Dwayne. Desi held Alicia on her shoulder, carefully gathered Anthony, and quickly followed.

When eventually she looked at the clock on the wall and saw she'd already been there an hour, she could scarcely believe it. One thing was sure—she didn't think she'd be bored working at ChildCare. She hugged Alicia, who bobbed her head and offered another sunny smile.

Desi quickly fell into a routine of working afternoons twice a week and every other Saturday at the house. Soon she couldn't imagine her life without Alicia and the other babies, and Tamara, Gayle, and Sadie. She shared enthusiastic stories about her af-

ternoons with her aunt and sometimes with Corrine.
Corrine didn't seem particularly interested, but she
listened politely. Desi tried to talk to her mother,
but she had become occupied with her job and
didn't appear to desire any details about Desi's
work. Since hunting season had started, her father
was gone every weekend, so he rarely had time to
hear what she had to tell either.

Desi wrote Valerie and was pleased when her
sister replied promptly:

*It sounds like you're having a great time. I'm
glad. Now that I'm at college, my high school
days seem so frivolous. Kids here discuss poli-
tics and social concerns. There are interest
groups for everything from saving the environment to feeding the world's starving. I wish I'd
done something more meaningful with my free
time the way you are. You'll fit into college life
real easy, sis.*

*Oh, thanks for the photo of baby Alicia. What a
doll! I know why you're crazy about her, and
it's a real downer that she may have to deal
with AIDS someday. Some guy in my English
class (150 students!) has AIDS from a blood
transfusion. Ted looks normal enough, but I understand he's doomed. It's scary. I wish I had
the nerve to strike up a conversation with him.*

*As for class life, it's hard. Trying to keep up my
grades AND keep my seeding on the tennis team
is really tough. I wish I had your brains!*

Love,
Val

*P.S. Don't worry about Mom. She'll come
around eventually. She's just concerned for
you.*"

Desi folded her sister's letter and wondered
how Val could ever be envious of her. Nevertheless,
Desi felt closer to her sister because she honestly
seemed to care about what Desi was doing. She'd be
glad when Thanksgiving came and Val would be
home. Maybe she could somehow arrange for Val to
meet Alicia. Desi smiled to herself and put her sister's letter away in her drawer of special keepsakes.

Desi was at her locker the morning Corrine
came up to her with a determined expression on her
face.

"Hi," Desi said, searching for a pencil.

Corrine held her books against her chest. "Are
you busy this weekend at that house with the AIDS
babies?"

"You know I am. Why?"

"Some girls from the pep club asked me to go to
the mall with them."

Desi wasn't very impressed with several of

those girls, but she didn't want to burst Corrine's bubble. "Sounds like you want to go."

Corrine nodded eagerly. "Of course I want to go. They don't let many freshmen hang around with them."

"Then go."

"I could ask them if you could come with us."

"Corrine, that's just not my thing."

"Well, I just wanted to give you a chance." Corrine shifted her books. "Guess I'll talk to you later."

"See you at lunch?"

"Not today. I'm sitting with my friends Sherry, Kristen, and Rebecca. Oh . . . and Randy Morris. I told you about him, remember?"

"No, I don't think you did."

"Well he's just a guy in my American studies class. He asked me out."

Desi knew how important having a date and a boyfriend was to her friend. "Corrine, that's terrific. You should have said something."

"You're so busy with that AIDS place, we hardly have any time to talk anymore. I'll tell you about Randy sometime when you're not so busy."

She wanted to tell Corrine to stop acting so childish. That it was all right for her to have other friends. Her own growing friendship with Tamara was helping her to see that it was possible to have a wide circle of friends and still care about old friends too. There was no need to feel joined at the hip to someone. "Maybe we can do something Sunday afternoon."

"Probably not. Randy's supposed to call me. Listen, I've got to go," Corrine called over her shoulder as she dashed down the hall.

Bewildered by Corrine's behavior, Desi fiddled aimlessly with her locker until she realized she was going to be late to class. She darted into biology just as the second bell rang, hurried to her lab table, and slid into her seat just as Mr. Redding started handing out yesterday's quiz papers. Desi noticed that Shaundra was absent, but Brian gave her a nod of greeting.

Around her kids shuffled and complained as they studied their quizzes. Brian Connley buried his face in his hands and moaned. Desi read her score, A+, and noticed Brian's D. For the life of her, she couldn't understand what was so difficult about biology.

From the front of the room Mr. Redding announced, "All of you know your assignment—dissecting your frogs." A few kids made faces. Mr. Redding told them, "Fill out the chart in your workbook as you dissect. I've got to step out for a few moments. Don't fool around. Get to work."

He left, and murmuring started. Desi lifted the frog out of the formaldehyde, stretched it out in the dissecting pan, and proceeded to slice it open. "Here, pin its skin flaps back, Brian," she directed. "That way we can expose the alimentary canal."

When he did nothing, she stole a glance at him. His face was the color of paste. "What's wrong?"

He stared at the slit-open frog. "Nothing."

"You look sick."

"Thanks. I love you too."

"Well, you do."

Suddenly Brian stood. "If Redding misses me, just tell him I skipped." He bolted for the door before Desi could say anything. Embarrassed, she shrugged to the kids around her. Two girls at the next table gave her mean looks.

Desi felt her face flush scarlet. What was wrong? Did she have lipstick on her teeth? Before she could check it out, Mr. Redding came back into the room. He glanced around and then said, "Desila, I'd like to see you up here please."

She caught an instantaneous case of bad nerves. Had she done something wrong? Had he noticed that Brian was gone, and would she have to lie for him? Heart pounding, she went to Redding's desk. "Yes, sir?"

"Desila, I've just gotten an official notice from the front office that Shaundra and her parents have requested a change of lab partners immediately. Can you think of any reason why she'd suddenly want to trade in one of the best biology students in my class?"

Chapter Six

⌒⌒

"No, sir," Desi told him, absolutely shocked by Mr. Redding's question.

"You two didn't have a falling out, did you?"

"Not that I know about."

Mr. Redding tapped his pencil against the top of his desk. "Well, all I know is that her parents went to the administration and asked for her to be moved, and I have to honor that request. So I guess it's just you and Mr. Connley.

"You know, I structure this course so you kids can learn how to work interactively. Your group was short a member from the first, and now you've lost another member. Let's hope Mr. Connley sticks it out, or I'll have to insert you into another group, which I don't want to do, because it will disturb *its* balance."

Desi was hardly listening. She kept trying to figure out why Shaundra would have asked to dump her as a lab partner. When the bell rang, she blended into the flow of the hall traffic, slipped into the bathroom, and checked her face in the mirror. "Same old me," she mumbled.

She was standing at her bus stop, waiting for

her school bus, when Brian pulled up in a rattling old car, flung open the door, and said, "Come on, I'll give you a lift."

No boy had ever offered her a ride home before. Desi got in, and Brian threw the car into gear and squealed out of the parking lot. She gripped the armrest.

"Did Redding miss me?" Brian asked.

"If he did, he didn't say anything in class."

A block later, Brian drove into a McDonald's parking lot, parked, and jumped out of the car. "Come on, I'm starved. I'll buy you a snack."

She hurried in after him and was sitting in a booth scowling out the window when he deposited the food on the table and sat down across from her. "So, what's with the long face?"

"Nothing."

"Did you get into trouble with Redding?"

"No."

"Well, something must have happened. Tell me."

She hesitated, but finally asked, "Did you know Shaundra asked to get out of being my lab partner?"

"Yeah, I heard."

She sat up straighter. "Does the whole school know? And why? What did I do to her?"

"The word's going around about you working with kids who have AIDS. I guess the idea sort of freaked her out."

Her jaw dropped. "But how——?" *Corrine.* Of

course. "A person can't catch AIDS just by being around people who have it."

"You and I know that," Brian said, "but that doesn't stop people from being scared."

"Well that's the stupidest, most juvenile thing I've ever heard. If people could just see these babies . . . Prejudice toward them is dumb! Stupid!"

"Hey, don't take it out on me."

"If I'm such a health risk, then why are *you* sitting across from me?"

He took a swig from his cup. "I guess because I'm not stupid and juvenile."

The clever way he turned her angry words made her smile. "Okay, so you're a good guy. But you can't go running out on me again like you did today. If you don't stick it out, who knows where Mr. Redding will put me?"

"I'll stick it out." Brian's intense blue eyes bore into hers, and for a moment her breath stuck in her throat.

"So tell me, why *did* you leave the room today?"

"It was the smell of that blasted dead frog and the junk it was soaking in."

"Formaldehyde." She studied him more closely. "What's the matter? You have a weak stomach or something?" He didn't answer, but leaned back against the booth and took a couple of deep breaths. "That's it," Desi pressed. "You're sick to your stomach even thinking about it."

"All right," Brian growled. "So I have a weak stomach. What's the big deal?"

"Well that's just terrific. I have one lab partner who dumps me because of where I spend my free time and another who tosses his cookies at the sight of frog guts."

Brian groaned. "Don't say that word. I might pass out." The idea of a macho guy like Brian fainting—coupled with the pasty color of his face—made her giggle. He gave her an imploring look. "Aw, have some mercy. Man, you don't know what it's like to be saddled with a weak stomach. I can't even go on roller coasters or Ferris wheels. It's grim."

"So that's why you never made it through biology last year?"

"I skipped every lab."

"We're going to have to work doubly hard in there now. There's just the two of us now."

"What if things get worse?"

"What do you mean? What things?"

"There are some kids at school who can make life pretty rough on you."

For a moment she felt baffled. "Are you saying some kids might be mean to me because I help out at ChildCare? Good grief! These are defenseless babies. Everybody knows about AIDS."

"Maybe some kids aren't as open-minded as you are," Brian said. "Maybe they can make you wish you never cared about AIDS babies either." A chill ran up her spine. Suddenly he offered a smile.

"Let's drop it. Besides, who'd be dumb enough to tangle with a girl who slashes frogs the way you do?"

She agreed with him and felt her mood improve. Outside, the long shadows of afternoon stretched across the parking lot. "I've got to get to work," he told her, stuffing the last of his fries in his mouth.

"Where do you work?"

"At a health club. I get to use the equipment, and it helps blow off steam. It's not a bad way to pass an afternoon if you need to."

"Are you telling me I might need to 'blow off steam'? But why?"

"It helps. Believe me—I speak from experience." She would have asked him more, but he stood and pulled her to her feet. His hand felt warm on hers. "Don't worry about the kids at school. Most are all right."

She recalled Alicia's elfin face. "I'm sorry there are people who feel threatened because I work at ChildCare. The babies are really special. And nobody wants them. No matter what happens or what anybody does, I'm not going stop helping with those babies."

The minute Desi walked into the ChildCare house the next Saturday, she recognized Alicia's crying. She hurried into the kitchen, where Sadie was walking the floor and juggling the screaming baby.

"What's wrong?" Concern made her heart pound crazily.

At the sound of Desi's voice Alicia turned her head and reached out her hand. Sadie handed the baby over. "She's cutting more teeth. Her gums must be hurting plenty; she's cried all morning."

Desi held Alicia close and rocked her. "There, there, baby girl," Desi cooed. "It's all right. I'm here now."

Sadie handed Desi a small tube of ointment. "Here's something to rub on her gums so they'll stop hurting." Desi sat in the rocker and proceeded to massage the numbing gel on the baby's gums. Alicia lay docilely, watching Desi. Sadie said, "That baby sure does like you, Desi. She just calms right down the minute she sees you or hears your voice."

Desi's heart swelled. Alicia *did* seem more responsive to her than to anyone else. She toyed with Alicia's hair, winding the soft ringlets around her finger. "She's a very special baby," Desi told Sadie. "And the fact that she likes me shows that she has excellent taste."

Sadie laughed. "I can tell that you've got things under control with that one, so I'll go check on Anthony. That boy's been sleeping all day long."

Desi dressed Alicia in a bonnet and sweater and took her for a walk on the grounds in a stroller. They were winding their way along a leaf-strewn path when she heard Tamara call, "Hey. I've been looking for you." Tamara came up alongside, holding Heather on her hip.

"Alicia needed some fresh air to keep her mind off her gums," Desi explained. The faint odor of burning leaves scented the crisp November air.

Tamara spread a small blanket out on the grass and plopped down with Heather. Desi lifted Alicia from the stroller and joined them on the cool grass. "So how's life in the salt mines?"

Desi told her about her conversation with Brian. Tamara listened, wide-eyed. "That's terrible. What are you going to do about it?"

"There's nothing I can do, except ignore it."

Tamara stroked Heather's arm. "Can you imagine what it's going to be like for these babies when they get into school? I mean, if they're lucky enough to live that long."

"It doesn't seem fair, does it? To have so much stacked against them."

"Maybe medical science will find a cure soon," Tamara added hopefully. "There's a lot of research going on, you know."

Desi touched Alicia's cheek. Her skin felt soft and warm, and the baby offered a sunny smile. "Maybe so."

Suddenly, from across the lawn, she heard Sadie calling their names and hurrying toward them. Desi scooped up Alicia. "What's wrong?" she asked as Sadie got closer.

"It's Anthony," Sadie said, her face dark with worry. "He's running a fever. I think he's pretty sick. I've just called an ambulance to take him to County Hospital."

Chapter Seven

"He's one sick baby," Aunt Clare said as she and Desi peered through the glass partition of the Pediatric Intensive Care Unit. Inside the cubicle Anthony lay in a crib with stainless steel bars. A feeding tube had been inserted in his nose and an IV line in his foot.

"But he'll be all right, won't he?" Desi asked.

"He's got thrush. In most infants it can be cleared up easily, but because Anthony's immune system isn't working properly, he's in bad shape. He's a tough little tyke though. Let's hope he can hang on until the antibiotics take hold."

Desi was scared. What if Anthony didn't get well? Gayle came alongside them, and Desi saw tight lines of concern around her mouth. "You'd think I'd be used to putting these babies back into the hospital by now. I never will." She shook her head sadly. "I've been on the phone all morning organizing volunteers to come in and be with him."

"Won't the nurses take care of him?" Desi asked.

"They'll care for his medical needs, but we don't want any of our babies to feel abandoned in the hospital. I mean, if he had a regular family, his mother would be with him; so we attempt to have someone with him around the clock. Someone he knows."

"But he's so out of it. How will he know anyone?"

"Even patients in comas respond to familiar voices. Sometimes a whopping dose of love can be more effective than all the hospital care in the world."

"That's true," Aunt Clare added. "When a child wakes up and sees a familiar face and is held in loving arms, his physical condition improves. Lots of studies have been done on the correlation between love and wellness. It's a fact that patients who are lovingly handled recover far more quickly than those who are simply given excellent medical care, but without additional stroking and touching."

"We want Anthony to have all the love and nurturing possible," Gayle said as she gazed through the glass. "I'm going to go be with him now for a while. Other volunteers will come in later." She went to the nurses' station and brought back a package marked 'Sterile' that contained a paper mask and gown, and slipped the gown over her clothes. Desi knew the precautions were to protect Anthony from additional germs.

Gayle patted Desi's hand. "Don't worry. Anthony will have plenty of attention while he's here in ICU. We don't want to neglect the others back at the house. We still need you to keep to your scheduled times with the children there."

"All right," she said. She wanted to stay with Anthony, but her real place was back at the house with Alicia. This couldn't happen to Alicia. Not to *her* baby.

Desi had an argument with her mother over her hanging around the hospital and spending extra hours at ChildCare. "I'm sorry, Desi," her mother told her as they worked in the kitchen, preparing supper, "but I'm having a really hard time understanding why you're so fixated on these potential AIDS babies. The whole idea truly bothers me."

"With Anthony sick, they need me more than ever."

"But you're being exposed to HIV on a daily basis."

"Mom, I'm not going to catch AIDS from the babies."

Her mother whirled from where she was washing vegetables at the sink. "But how do you *know* that? I know doctors say that people can only catch it under certain conditions, but what if they're wrong? What if the people who are 'helping' with today's HIV victims find out later that they've contracted AIDS?"

"Mom, ChildCare gets all the newest information about the AIDS virus. I read everything! Scientists have proven that the virus isn't very hardy. It can't survive without ideal growing conditions. Outside the body, household bleach can kill it."

"Don't feed me all that scientific mumbo-jumbo, Desi! It's you I'm concerned about. *You.* I'd never forgive myself if you caught this horrible disease. And all because of some babies you feel some misplaced sense of civic duty toward. I could just throttle Clare every time I think about how she's involved you in this."

Desi watched her mother's pinched, angry expression and felt confused. Why was she so against this project? She wished there was some sort of hookup from her heart to her mother's brain. Some way of instantly and painlessly revealing her deep feelings for Alicia and lack of fear for herself.

In a quiet voice Desi said, "It's not civic duty for me, Mom. It's much more than that. Every time I look at Alicia, every time I hold her, I don't want to let her go. I want to make all the bad things in her life go away. She's just a little baby, Mom. A tiny six-month-old baby.

"Her mother took drugs and gave HIV to her baby. It was her mother who did wrong, but it's Alicia who has to pay for it." Desi noticed her mother wince, as if her words were hurting her physically. What was her mother *really* thinking?

Desi hurriedly added, "Please don't blame Aunt Clare, Mom. I'm not good at tennis like Valerie. I'm never going to be a beauty queen the way you were, or popular, like Valerie is. I'm just me. Plain old Desila. I like what I'm doing at ChildCare."

Slowly her mother dried her hands on a dish towel, folded it methodically, and placed it on the counter. She looked away from Desi and as she walked toward the door, asked, "Can you finish up supper without me?"

Startled, confused by her mother's response, Desi replied, "Sure, I can. But—"

"Finish the salad, and when the buzzer goes off, take the roast out of the oven."

"Okay, but—"

"Warm the rice for you and your dad."

"Aren't you eating with us?"

Her mother shook her head. "No. I've got a headache. I'll take something and lie down before it gets worse."

"But, Mom—"

"It's all right, Desi. Please go on with your plans."

Dumbfounded, Desi watched her mother leave the kitchen. Something was wrong, something deeper than Desi's volunteer work. She hadn't a clue what it could be.

On Friday night Desi sat curled up in the corner of her aunt's sofa. She was spending the weekend at her aunt's again, since her father was on a hunting trip and her mother was attending a decorators' convention in New York. "How's Anthony doing today?"

"They removed his feeding tube because he's able to swallow on his own now. They're hoping to discharge him and send him back to the house after Thanksgiving," Aunt Clare called from the kitchen.

"That's super," Desi called in return.

Outside, a cold November rain was falling. Desi snuggled closer into the sofa cushion as her aunt entered the room, carrying a snack tray. "You know, I'm *really* looking forward to Valerie's coming home for Thanksgiving next week. I think Mom needs to see her."

"What makes you say that?"

"She's acting strange about my volunteer work. Whenever Val's at home, Mom seems happier. I think Mom misses Val more than she let's on. They have so much in common—Mom kind of lights up whenever she's with Val, and you know that's the truth."

Aunt Clare set the tray down on the glass-topped cocktail table and handed Desi a cup of hot chocolate. "Tell me, how is your mother acting strange?"

"It's the AIDS thing, I guess. I thought she was over it, but she and I got into it again the other night. I told Val about it a while back, and she said that Mom would eventually come around, but I'm not so sure. I'm starting to think that it's something more than AIDS."

"More? What do you mean?"

"I'm not sure, but I know something else is bothering her." Desi licked a dollop of whipped cream floating atop her chocolate and wished she could define her impressions more clearly. "I have this brainstorm that might give her some peace of mind about my work. Would you like to hear it?"

"I'm all ears."

"I thought I could do my science fair project about AIDS. I have to discuss it with Brian first—he's my lab partner. I figured if we could present facts and statistics about AIDS, the information might calm Mom down some. What do you think?"

Aunt Clare beamed Desi a smile. "I think you're a wonderful, thoughtful daughter."

"It's just an idea. I mean, I have to do a science project anyway, so—why not? Of course I'll have to talk Brian into it, but he's been pretty understanding about my 'fixation' on the ChildCare house—as Mom calls it."

"Have you said anything to your dad about your mother's fears?"

"No . . . He's so busy all the time. When he is home, he falls asleep in front of the TV. Do you think I should say something?"

Aunt Clare pursed her lips. "Maybe not yet. Let's see how she is after Val visits. And you're right —maybe a science fair project that spells everything out will help."

Desi nodded thoughtfully, wishing that her mother were as easy to relate to as her aunt.

On Monday morning Desi climbed off the school bus and headed for her locker. She was glad that Thanksgiving break was only three days away. She needed time away from the vibes and undercurrents she kept feeling at school.

She had almost reached her locker when she noticed kids pointing at her and whispering. The back of her neck tingled. Why had she suddenly become the topic of conversation? At her locker she stopped and stared. Spray-painted red letters left a hateful message: "Get Out, Nigger Queer Lover."

Chapter Eight

Too shocked to move, Desi stared, but the shock gave way to horror, and horror to fear. She backed away, turned, and ran, shoving past people, struggling to keep her tears inside.

She hit the main entrance and raced down the steps. She ran until her lungs burned and her legs felt rubbery. She stopped at a corner and willed her heart to cease pounding. All around her, morning traffic flowed. The rest of the world appeared perfectly normal.

She wondered what to do. She couldn't go back to school, and she had no way to get home. As she dug into her purse, looking for bus fare, a car pulled up at the curb. She recognized the rumble of the broken muffler instantly. "Get in," Brian said, leaning across the seat and opening the door.

She didn't need an invitation, and jumped inside. "Did—did you see my locker?" she asked haltingly as he pulled out into traffic.

"I just heard about it."

She buried her face in her hands. "Why would someone do that? Why would someone write those awful words?"

"Because some people are stupid and mean. And gutless too. You can't pay any attention to idiots like that."

"But how can they hate me so much? They don't even know me." She fumbled for a tissue.

"The operative word is *hate*, Desi. Hate has its own agenda and doesn't need a reason."

"I've heard about hate groups, but I never expected to run into one in high school."

"Grady has a couple of them. People who hate everyone who's different—blacks, gays, any minority —it doesn't matter. They're misguided jerks who spout 'ethnic purity' and have no tolerance for anyone who's different from them. I think it's a disease worse than AIDS."

"Ethnic purity"—he used a term she'd read in history books and heard occasionally on the nightly news. Until now the phrase had had no meaning, but all at once she saw it in all its ugliness. She found a tattered tissue in her purse and blew her nose. "Do these kids really think I'm going to give them AIDS because I volunteer at the ChildCare house?"

"Probably not, but it is a scary disease. Fear makes people do dumb things." Brian pulled into a parking place beside a public park. "Come on, let's walk."

Her legs felt shaky, but she walked with him. They crossed the grass and stopped at a pond where ducks swam on murky, sun-studded water. A cool breeze dried the dampness on her cheeks. Desi felt tired and completely drained. "It's hard to believe kids like us belong to hate groups."

"Believe it," Brian said. "But you can't spend your life looking over your shoulder, wondering if someone's going to grab you."

Until he mentioned it, the idea hadn't crossed her mind. "Do you think someone might try and hurt me?"

"I don't think so. People like that use fear as their biggest weapon. They use scare tactics because they're cowards."

"Well, their tactics are working," Desi confessed. She glanced sideways, saw his rugged profile, his muscular build and long hair, and recalled that the first time she'd met him she'd been slightly fearful of him. Then another thought occurred to her. "How do you know so much about these hate groups?"

"I'm blond and blue-eyed. The perfect candidate for racial purity." He laughed mirthlessly. "I told them all to leave me alone, that I wasn't interested."

Overwhelmed by all that had happened that morning, Desi suddenly thought of her mother's world of high school innocence. Had that kind of world vanished altogether? "So you think I should ignore the message on my locker?"

"If you don't ignore it, then they've got you where they want you."

"I don't want to play by their rules," Desi told

him with more courage than she felt. "And I won't give up my volunteer work."

He took her by the elbow and turned her to face him. "If people would only use their brains, they'd realize that the medical types at that house aren't going to let you be around something that's hazardous to your health. I mean, they wouldn't knowingly risk a lawsuit now, would they?"

Desi agreed with him. What Brian said made perfect sense.

"And I'm sure that your parents wouldn't let you do something that might be harmful to you either."

"My mom's sort of been hassling me," she confessed.

"Hassling is what moms do best," Brian said with a grin.

"Maybe we could do our science fair project about AIDS," Desi suggested. "I can get all the information we need from ChildCare, so no long hours of being stuck in the library doing basic research. I'll bet it'll score points with Mr. Redding. Practically a guaranteed A."

"I'm not so sure I want to do a project about AIDS."

"Why not?"

"Hey, don't take it personally. I don't want to do *any* science project. I've got my job on top of my studies, and I don't want to overextend myself."

"Not even for an A? You said you *had* to pass this year."

"We are passing. Your surgical skills slicing open frogs, my neat, organized journal keeping—we've got this course down cold. All I want is to pass the thing."

"But a project—"

"Forget it. We can make it fine without all the extra-credit work."

She was disappointed. For a time she'd thought they'd been on the same wavelength, that they'd shared some deep understanding about life. Now she saw that except for his explanation about organized hate groups, Brian was just a lazy student. He was content to slide by, and there was nothing she could say to motivate him.

They stood at the edge of the pond in an awkward silence. The sun warmed the back of Desi's neck and shoulders. "So now what?" he asked. "Where do you want to go? Back to school?"

"No. I can't go back there today."

"Home?"

"Not there either." She didn't want to tell him that she hated the thought of being alone all day. "If Mom finds out about the hate message, she'll make me give up going to ChildCare for sure."

"So where?"

She turned to face him. "Will you take me to ChildCare? Maybe I can help out today and get my mind off this whole thing. If you take me, I'll introduce you to Alicia."

"Who's she?"

Desi smiled mysteriously. "It's a surprise. But I will tell you this—she's drop-dead beautiful."

"Thank heavens you're here," Sadie said the moment Desi and Brian arrived. "Two of our regulars phoned in sick with the flu, and our backup helper is staying with Anthony at the hospital this morning."

Desi introduced an obviously self-conscious Brian, then asked, "Where's Alicia?"

"Just stirring from her morning nap. Maybe you could bathe her."

Desi seized Brian's arm and dragged him down the hall into the sunny yellow bedroom that Alicia and Heather shared. Alicia was lying in her crib, babbling to herself and kicking at the slats. When Desi leaned over, the baby's face lit up, and she reached her arms upward. Desi scooped her up and hugged her close. "This is Alicia," Desi cooed, holding Alicia toward Brian, who shifted from foot to foot. "Isn't she adorable?"

The baby seemed to study him, then swatted the air and buried her face in Desi's neck. Desi laughed. "Do you always have that effect on women?"

"Very funny. I prefer my women a little older, that's all."

"Come on. You can watch me give her a bath."

"Are you kidding?" He shifted nervously. "I've got to go to work."

"School's not even out yet. You've got time." She went to Alicia's dresser and sorted through clean clothes with one hand while she held the baby in her other arm. "You could give me a hand, you know." She smiled at Brian. "Trust me. It'll be fun."

He came over and halfheartedly picked through the jumble of baby clothes. "How do I know what goes together?" He found a white nylon sock trimmed in yellow and another trimmed in pale green.

"That's not a fashion statement, Brian."

"I know that." He dug through the drawer until he discovered the mate to the yellow one.

Desi marched into the bathroom and drew a few inches of warm water into the tub. Quickly she stripped Alicia and sat her in the water. The baby squealed with delight, slapped the water with her feet and hands, and sent sprays all over the front of Brian, who was hovering over the tub.

He yelped, and Desi giggled. Alicia laughed, clapped her pudgy hands together, and slapped the water again. In minutes the water was puddling on the floor. Brian wailed, "Help me! I'm melting! I'm melting!" just like the witch in *The Wizard of Oz.*

Desi laughed while Alicia kept splashing and squealing.

After the bath Desi put Alicia in her high chair and fed her. Brian sat in the rocker and watched. He said, "She doesn't look like a health hazard, does she?"

Soberly Desi spooned strained apricots into Alicia's dainty mouth. "She's just a sweet little baby who never did anything to hurt anybody. It doesn't seem right that people can hate her just because she *might* get AIDS."

"Yeah, it's a shame all right." He stood. "Look, I need to split."

Surprised by his abruptness, Desi missed Alicia's mouth. "Thanks for helping me out today."

"Well, I've never bathed a baby before."

"That's not what I mean. Thanks for the ride from school. For being there for me."

"Will you be okay to go back tomorrow?"

"What's a little paint on a locker?" She tried to sound cheerful, but inside she was scared.

"If it'll make you feel better, I can wait for you at the main door and walk with you to biology. I mean, we *are* partners."

"I'd like that." He left, and Desi cleaned Alicia up and sat with her in the rocking chair. "He's a nice guy," she whispered to the baby nestled in her arms, feeling some need to explain why she liked having Brian around. "And he needs me to pass biology." Alicia's eyelids drooped. Her small hand clutched the front of Desi's blouse. "And he's *too* muscular for my tastes." The baby slept. "Honest, he's definitely not my type."

Desi gazed down at Alicia's face, at the sweep of lashes that almost brushed her cheek, at her tiny, perfect lips, at her smooth and flawless brown skin. She smelled of baby powder and clean soap. "I love you, Alicia," Desi whispered. She bent and pressed her cheek against the baby's forehead. "And I'll always be here for you. No matter how hatefully other people behave."

She rose and walked the baby to her crib, where she laid her down on her stomach and covered her with a flannel blanket adorned with pink elephants and yellow ducks. Desi's heart ached with love. She didn't care how bad things got at school, how mean, how threatening. She would never abandon Alicia. The way the baby's mother had.

Chapter Nine

~⁓~

Desi met Brian at the entrance the next morning and walked beside him to her locker. To her relief she saw that the janitorial staff had removed all traces of the red paint. When the principal made a short speech about the consequences of defacing school property during morning announcements, Desi felt anxious. She hadn't been called in to the front office and assumed that the administration was dealing with the incident as an act of vandalism, not an attack on Desila Mitchell.

Over the next week no one at school had much to do with Desi, except for Brian. She told herself she'd never been popular anyway and it didn't matter—but it *did*. Especially with Corrine. Her long-time friend's abandonment hurt Desi. "I'm telling you, Randy takes all my time," Corrine insisted.

"Then I guess you'll be too busy to see much of me over the holiday."

"I guess so," Corrine replied without meeting Desi's eyes.

Desi's hurt turned to anger as she asked herself, *Who needs Corrine Johnson anyway?* "Well, don't eat too much turkey. See you around." Desi left Corrine standing in the hall.

That afternoon, when Desi went over to Child-Care, Sadie was upset. "It's Anthony," Sadie explained.

"I thought he might be home for Thanksgiving."

"We all thought so, but he's taken a turn for the worse."

Desi felt as if an icy hand had squeezed her heart. She had a flood of questions, but before she could ask any, Gayle asked to speak with her privately. Nervously Desi followed her into the living room. The second they sat down on the sofa, she blurted, "Is something wrong?"

"Yes," Gayle said bluntly. "You've read our guidelines for volunteers, haven't you?"

"Sure."

"Then you know our rules state that family members and friends of volunteers should not accompany them here." Desi nodded. "Sadie tells me that you brought a friend with you the other day. She didn't say anything to you at the time because she was so shorthanded. I told her she should have."

Desi was ashamed of herself. How could she have forgotten such an important rule? What if Gayle told her she couldn't be a volunteer anymore? "I'm sorry. I had a bad experience at school that morning, and I didn't know where else to go. Brian brought me here, and I introduced him to Alicia. We got to playing with her, and I just didn't think. I'm really sorry."

Gayle looked earnestly at Desi. "I'm sure your friend is a perfectly fine person, but we have rules for everyone's safety. The whole point of ChildCare is to give the babies a consistent, stable home life. We don't want strangers around them. It causes confusion and breaks into the daily routine."

"It won't happen again."

"Plus, you know how careful we have to be about the babies' being around sick people. Especially now with Anthony so sick. We're all on guard against germs."

It hadn't occurred to her that Brian might be harboring germs he could have passed on to the babies. "I would never do anything to hurt them."

"Of course you wouldn't. You're an excellent helper." Gayle pressed her fingertips against her temples and sighed. "I'm not picking on you, Desi. It's just that today's been hard for me. We may lose Anthony. I never get used to watching a child die. Whenever I lose one, I ask, 'Why? Why do the innocent suffer?' "

She glanced over at Desi. "I'm sorry," Gayle said. "No one has those answers. In the end I always pull myself together and vow to help all the others. Thank you for caring enough to want to help these babies too."

Desi swallowed a lump in her throat. "Nothing's more important to me than Alicia." When

Gayle said nothing, Desi added, "The others too. I love them all. I want Anthony to get well more than anything! I'm sure he will."

Gayle took Desi's hands in hers. Desi hoped they didn't feel as cold and clammy to Gayle as they did to her. "Desi, I know that you're attached to Alicia, but you do understand her situation, don't you?"

"Sure I do."

"She might develop AIDS at any time."

"Well, of course, but—"

Gayle interrupted. "There is no cure for AIDS."

"Nothing's going to happen to Alicia. She's never been sick." Desi stood and paced to the window. Outside, fallen leaves in faded autumn colors were scattered over the browning lawn. "I'm real sorry that I broke the rules and let Brian come into the house. I'll never do it again."

Gayle walked over and hugged Desi's shoulders. "We can always use extra help—if he wants to help out—but he'll have to go through the training program just like everyone else."

"I don't think this is Brian's thing. He was just doing me a favor."

"All right—enough said. I know you'll be more careful in the future." Gayle smiled, assuring Desi that the reprimand was behind them. Together they returned to the kitchen. Alicia was with Sadie, but she raised her arms toward Desi the moment she saw her. Desi lifted the baby and cuddled her closely, trying not to be afraid for her. Trying hard to forget that she was HIV-positive and at risk for AIDS.

Valerie rode home from college with two other students from Atlanta late Wednesday night. All her suitcases and duffel bags were stuffed full. "No laundry facilities in Gainesville?" her father joked as he lugged her things into the house.

"Oh, Daddy!" She hugged her parents and turned to hug Desi. "I like the way you're wearing your hair," Valerie said.

Desi was pleased. She'd been growing her hair long since school started, but Val was the only one who'd noticed.

Mom held Val tightly. "It's good to have you back home. We've missed you so much, honey."

"But, Mom, it's only been three months."

Her mother held Val at arm's distance and studied her with glowing eyes. "Are you eating enough? You look thin."

Val rolled her eyes. "Mother!"

Desi laughed, but she had to admit that Val did look much thinner.

Dad interrupted. "Eva, at least let Val get settled in before you start making her over." He started up the stairs with the baggage.

"I've got turkey and all the trimmings for tomorrow." Their mother linked her arm through Valerie's and started up the stairs behind him. "And Friday the department stores open as early as eight in the morning, so we'll hit all the malls. We've got so much to do and only a weekend to do it in."

"I'll be home for Christmas," Val said as her mother continued talking, but she cast a long-suffering look over her shoulder toward Desi. Desi tagged along behind them, wondering if she'd ever be greeted so happily when *she* came home from college in the years ahead.

Aunt Clare arrived early Thanksgiving morning to help Eva and Desi with the meal. Desi pulled her to one corner, out of her mother's earshot and asked about Anthony. Her aunt shook her head. "The news isn't good. He's fighting a viral pneumonia. Let's make sure to include him in our Thanksgiving prayers."

Desi nodded and quickly set to work, hoping that by keeping busy, she could put Anthony's plight out of her mind. When everything was ready, Desi stood and admired the table. Her mother's decorating skills were evident.

China, crystal, and silver sparkled on ivory-color linen. The colors of autumn spilled from a magnificent brass and straw centerpiece of fall flowers, gourds, pheasant feathers, and candles. The rich, succulent aroma of roasted turkey, yeast rolls, cinnamon, and spiced pumpkin pies saturated the air. With the strains of a Rachmaninoff concerto playing on the stereo, and late afternoon sunlight spilling

through antique lace curtains, the room had the fla-
vor of some turn-of-the-century Southern mansion.

"Beautiful," Aunt Clare announced when they
all finally sat down to dine.

As her father blessed the food, Desi prayed si-
lently for Anthony, for his fight for life. She thought
about Alicia too, and wondered what it would be like
to have her sitting in a high chair at their table. Desi
could picture her small hand holding a drumstick
and her dark eyes glowing. Maybe next year she
could talk Gayle into letting her bring Alicia over for
the day. If her mother would agree to such a venture.

"It's so wonderful to have my family together,"
her mother declared, passing around the food.

"It's good to take a break," Val volunteered. Her
hair was tied back with a blue satin ribbon, her
freshly scrubbed face pretty, as always, but pale. She
turned toward Desi, asking, "Tell me about the
ChildCare house you've written about. Your letters
are great. Can I go see the babies with you? I'd love
to see more pictures too."

Filled with enthusiasm, Desi started to speak,
but her mother interrupted. "Oh, Val, honey, your
father and I hear about Desi's activities all the time.
We want to hear about yours. Do you like your
classes? How's tennis coming along? I can't wait until spring. According to your coach, Florida plays
several matches here in Atlanta. You can bet we'll all
be there to cheer you on."

Desi felt the sting of her mother's rejection. She saw a flare of anger in her aunt's eyes, but before Aunt Clare could comment and set off an argument, Desi said, "Come on, Val, tell us all about what you're doing. You and I can talk later about my life."

Valerie began to tell stories of campus life, hesitantly at first, then more excitedly. Desi found her sister's stories amusing, but she kept wishing her mother was as interested in her activities as she appeared to be in Val's.

Much later, when they were clearing the table and loading the dishwasher together, Val told her, "I really want us to have a long talk, Desi, and hear about everything you're doing. I don't think Mom really meant to cut you off, you know."

"Probably not. She's still not crazy about my working at ChildCare, and she really has missed you a lot."

"Too bad you're not the older of us," Val said with a sigh.

"Why do you say that?"

"Because then everybody would expect *you* to be perfect. It's the curse of being firstborn, you know. My roommate and I talk about it all the time. She's a firstborn too."

Desi wanted to tell her, "But you *are* perfect!" Instead she asked, "Aren't you having a good time in college?"

"Oh sure, but I feel under so much pressure. I have to be a good student *and* a great athlete. Coach is always urging me to practice and 'be committed.' The competition is fierce on the team and in my classes. My professors keep telling me that I could do so much better if only I'd study more. Mom's always calling and writing telling me how important it is that I have a good four years at Florida if I want to do something 'serious' with tennis." Valerie threw up her hands in exasperation. "Honestly, sometimes I feel like dumping everything. I envy you. Still going to high school without any problems."

She'd never written Val about the episode at school, and now didn't seem like a good time to mention it. "But you love tennis. I thought you wanted to turn pro."

"I *do* love it. But I'm not sure I want it to be my whole life." Valerie bent over the open dishwasher and slowly inserted the plates Desi was handing her. "Still I know that Mom's put a lot of herself into my game and that it matters to her that I excel." Val straightened. "Sometimes I wish Mom and Dad hadn't gotten married right after high school. If Mom had gone to college, played tennis, and lived a little, I'll bet she'd be different now. Sometimes I feel like I'm doing things for her instead of me."

She looked at Desi and quickly added, "Don't get me wrong. I'm glad I'm on scholarship, and I honestly love the game. It's just that sometimes . . ." She shrugged helplessly. "Oh, forget it. I sound like I'm complaining, and I'm not. Just take my word for it—life's tough."

Desi didn't have to be reminded of that. "Maybe you should say something to Mom."

"No. I don't think she'd understand."

"She's really into her decorating job," Desi insisted. "It's important to her, she's so concerned about everything you do, I bet she could relate to your feelings about tennis not being your whole life."

"It's more complicated than that. I like the competition, and I like winning. I *really* like winning. It's just that right now I'm having trouble figuring out exactly what I want and how to get it. You understand, don't you?"

Desi nodded solemnly. She understood perfectly. Each of them had problems. Val had their mother's great expectations resting on her, and Desi felt that her parents expected nothing much from her at all. She began to think about the baby her parents had lost and wished she knew more about him and what had happened. Too bad he was never discussed. She couldn't help wondering what things would have been like if that baby had lived. What would have been expected of him, the only boy? How different would their family have been with him alive? They would never know.

Desi watched Val pour detergent into the dishwasher and turn on the machine. No matter how bad things were for Val and herself, Desi knew that their problems weren't as bad as Alicia's. And Alicia didn't even have a family, anyone to love her. *That's not so,* Desi reminded herself. *She* loved Alicia, and no matter how terrible things got for either of them, she would *always* be there for baby Alicia.

Chapter Ten

Desi stood in the food court area of the giant mall, plotting her shopping strategy. She wasn't due to hook up with Valerie and her mother again until four o'clock, so that meant she'd have plenty of time to find everyone's Christmas gifts. She studied her list. Aunt Clare was first. In Neiman Marcus she found a small colorful ceramic elephant for her aunt's collection. As she was paying, she heard someone call her name.

"I thought that was you," Brian Connley said after he'd cut through a group of shoppers. "What're you doing here?" He was slightly out of breath.

"Is this a trick question? I'm shopping, of course."

"Did you get my present yet?"

"Golly, I almost forgot. Good thing you reminded me."

He fell into step beside her. "Mind if I tag along? Maybe you could help me pick out some things for my mom and sister."

"I don't know your mom and sister."

"So what? You're all *females*. You must have some idea of what girls want." With his wayward blond hair and big blue eyes, he looked too appealing to refuse. "I'll buy you lunch," he offered as a bribe.

She was glad to be with him, she just didn't want him to know it. "All right, but you've got to help me get the stuff on my list. No whining, even if you get bored."

"Me? It'll never happen."

She led him over to the perfume counter. "Does your mom like any special scent?"

"Eau de hamburger," he suggested with a grin.

"Be serious."

He studied the bottles, lifted one, and saw the price. "Do I look like a millionaire? Forget this."

They passed through several more departments before Brian could be persuaded to part with some of his money. He bought his mother a silk scarf that Desi assured him anyone would like. While he was paying, Desi gazed across the aisle and noticed the children's department. Quickly she walked in that direction. In the center of the toddler area she saw a red velvet dress trimmed in white eyelet lace at the neck and sleeves, with a white organdy bow at the waist.

"It's a little small, don't you think?" Brian asked, as he sauntered over with his package.

"It's the most beautiful thing I've ever seen!" Desi cried, ignoring his remark. She stroked the nap of the plush velvet.

"So who's it for?"

"Did you take leave of your brain? Alicia, of course!"

"You're buying a *baby* a Christmas present? What for?"

"Because I want her to have it. She should have something special on Christmas Day."

"What's the matter with a rattle or a doll?"

Desi rolled her eyes in exasperation. "I'll get her something like that too, but this is—is—" She groped for words. "Oh never mind. Just imagine her in this dress. She'll look precious. I can get her some of those lacy white socks to match and maybe a red velvet bow for her hair."

He flipped over the sales tag and let out a low whistle. "You're going to have to rob a bank to pay for it."

She fingered the tag and swallowed hard. It *was* very expensive and would take a chunk of her Christmas money. Her mind raced. Maybe she could make something for her grandparents—Grandma would rather have something homemade anyway. And she could pick up a house plant for her mother and a wicker basket to put it in . . . She held the dress higher. "I'm going to get it for Alicia. It's *too* perfect to pass up."

"Well if you want my opinion—"

"No thanks." Desi stepped around him and found white lace tights instead of socks. She paid for everything at the register while Brian made himself scarce. She was looking for him when he came up behind her.

"Here. Give her this from me." Brian thrust a small bag into her hand.

"What is it?" She opened the bag and pulled out a plush, stuffed frog. "This is for Alicia?" His generosity touched her.

"To help make up for all the frogs we've dismembered in biology."

She laughed. "*Who* dismembered?"

"All right, all right, O great scalpel wielder." He bowed elaborately from the waist. "Anyway, a new dress is okay, but I think she needs something to cuddle. Actually everyone does, you know."

Christmas music floated above them. Beautiful displays sparkled with holiday colors from every countertop, and crowds of people swirled around them, but for a moment, looking into Brian's eyes, Desi felt they were the only two people in the busy store. Her heartbeat quickened. "Where to next?" Brian asked.

"I thought of something else I want to get for Alicia," she said, seeing a notation she'd made on her list. "We'll find it in a card shop."

"You're going to give her a Christmas card?" Brian questioned, bewildered. "I *know* she can't read yet."

"No, silly. I'm going to get her a baby book."

"What's that?"

She worked her way through the crowds in the

mall toward the nearest store specializing in cards and stationery. Brian dogged her steps. "It's a book that records stuff about your baby—weight, length, tooth-cutting info, first words, steps—that sort of stuff."

"Oh yeah," he said. "My mom has one of those for me. What are they good for?"

"Maybe she'll want to know all those things about herself someday."

"But shouldn't her mother be writing those things down?"

"I don't know anything about her mother except that she abandoned Alicia. I doubt she'd do much for her baby book."

"Yes, but—"

"But nothing. I'm keeping a baby book for her, and that's that."

Brian shrugged. "You don't have to bite my head off."

"Sorry." Desi realized she shouldn't have grown so irritated with him. He was trying to be helpful. How could she expect him to understand her feelings for Alicia? She came to a shelf filled with keepsake books and leafed through several. "What do you think of this one?" She held it up for Brian's inspection.

"Cute teddy bears," he told her, all the while studying her.

"I like it best," she announced, feeling uncomfortable under his gaze. "Let me pay for it, then you can buy me that lunch you promised."

At the food court Desi sat with the packages, watching shoppers bustle past, while Brian bought food. Desi saw Corrine among a group of girls, laughing and talking. She recalled the hours and hours she'd spent over the years with her former best friend. Corrine was purposely avoiding her. She never called anymore, and they rarely spoke at school. Quickly Desi averted her head, not wanting the girls to see her sitting alone.

"Do you have much shopping left to do?" Brian asked when he returned, balancing a tray.

"Just my dad and sister, Valerie. What're you buying your dad?"

"Nothing. My parents are divorced, and Dad lives in California with his new family." He handed her a cup of diet cola and a paper plate filled with pizza.

"Do you ever see him?"

"I haven't since I was seven."

She couldn't imagine not seeing her father. True, he wasn't around all that much, but at least she knew he was coming home every night. "So you grew up with only women bossing you around?" Desi teased.

"Not quite."

Desi waited for him to continue, but after an awkward moment it became obvious that he was finished talking about his personal life. She fidgeted self-consciously with her shopping bag and finally took another peek at Alicia's new dress. "Alicia's really going to look pretty in this."

Brian blew the paper off his straw and jammed it through the lid of his cup. "You sure act funny about that baby."

"What do you mean?"

"You act like she's your kid or something."

"I do not."

"You sure do. Remember, I was with you and saw the way you treat her. And now you've bought her all these presents."

"She's special to me, that's all." Desi knew she sounded defensive. Brian obviously didn't understand.

"But what about the other babies at the house? You didn't mess with them at all that day I took you."

"I do lots of things with the others. You're not around me all the time, so how would you know?" she asked between bites of pizza.

"I'm just telling you how it *looks*, Desi. Just be careful, because you might be setting yourself up for a fall."

"Like what? She'll get sick? Don't you think I know that? I'll still love her, even if she does."

"Sometimes love isn't enough." Brian wadded his napkin and tossed it over her head, toward the trash container.

"How'd you get to be such an expert on love?"

All around them shoppers passed, juggling

packages and boxes, and the smells of food mingled with the scents of bayberry and evergreen. "I don't know dip about love, but I know a lot about giving it to the wrong people," he said seriously.

Was he telling her about his father or maybe an old girlfriend? She disliked the thought of another girl in his life. "What wrong people?"

"Nothing. Forget I said anything." Brian leaned down and scooped up his purchases. "Let's go. You promised to help me find something for my sister."

"I said I would, didn't I? Maybe we can get her a gift in the bookstore. Does your sister like to read?" Desi scrambled for her belongings, half grateful to switch the subject. Maybe she'd been foolish to pry into his personal life. After all, he was only her biology lab partner. What he did and whom he cared about was none of her business. Just as it was none of his business how she felt for Alicia.

Chapter Eleven

"Want to see some of the presents I bought to-day?" Desi asked. Now that they were home from the mall, she stood at the doorway of Valerie's bedroom, clutching her shopping bag.

Val sat on the floor wrapping an oversize box. "You can come in—it's safe. I've already wrapped yours and stashed it in my closet." She waggled her finger. "No peeking after I go back to school."

Desi sat cross-legged on the floor. "It's been fun having you home for Thanksgiving. I wish you could stay longer."

"I'll be back in a few weeks for Christmas break." Val tacked a bow onto the foil-wrapped box in front of her and shoved it to one side. "Who was the hunk you were with today? I saw you from a distance walking with him, but you were so involved, you didn't see me."

"Just some guy from school. His name's Brian."

Valerie arched one perfect black eyebrow. "Have you been holding back information from me, little sister?"

The teasing tone of her voice made Desi blush.

"I was helping him do his Christmas shopping. He's nothing to me. Really."

"I was wondering when your hormones would override that scientifically splendid brain of yours."

"Val! He's just a friend."

Valerie chuckled. "I love seeing you squirm."

Desi playfully tossed a wad of ribbon at her sister. "Do you want to see the things I bought today, or not?" Val nodded, and Desi pulled the items she bought Alicia from the sack.

"Wow!" Val fingered the plush velvet of the dress. "This is gorgeous."

"I can't wait to see Alicia in it."

"You're really crazy about this little girl, aren't you?"

"She's so darling, Val. I can't help myself." Desi folded the dress lovingly and placed it inside a box. "I'm telling you, the time I spend down at Child-Care is the best time of my life. You always had tennis, but I've never had anything that meant as much to me. I just wish Mom could be more understanding about it."

"Actually I think she wants me to try to persuade you to give it up."

Desi looked up quickly. "Don't even bother. I'll never leave Alicia."

"Maybe you should put yourself in Mom's place."

"Maybe she should put herself in *my* place," Desi countered.

"Aren't you afraid of AIDS?"

"Are you afraid of that guy in your class who has AIDS?" Desi watched her sister's slender fingers roll ribbon back onto a spool.

"I feel sorry for Ted, but I am a little bit scared whenever I'm around him. It's not a rational fear," she added when Desi started to protest. "It's a deep-down, dark kind of fear. I wish I weren't afraid. But I know what this guy's future is. I've seen pictures of people in advanced stages of AIDS, and it's pretty grim. Ted still keeps trying to lead a regular life though. He goes to classes, he has his own apartment off campus. He has a few friends. Once in the student union I caught him staring at me. He looked so sad."

"You can talk to him and be his friend. You don't have to date him or anything," Desi urged, feeling sympathetic.

Val shook her head. "I'm no good at hiding my feelings. He'll always know that I'm really feeling revulsion. I'm sorry. I wish I felt differently, but I don't."

"Well, I'm not afraid," Desi insisted.

"I admire you."

Val's admission took Desi by surprise. She was the one who'd always envied and admired Val. Self-consciously she shifted, grabbed up her sack, and pulled out another gift. "See what else I got Alicia."

"A baby book! Oh, Desi, how cute." Val ran her palm over the pale pink cover. "Look at the teddy bears." She thumbed through the stiff, decorated pages. "How will you know what to fill in about Alicia's birth statistics?"

"Alicia was born at County Hospital, so between Gayle and Aunt Clare I think I can get the info I need."

"You know what might be fun? Let's drag out our old baby books and see what Mom wrote in them."

"I've never seen them. Do you know where they are?"

Val drummed her fingers. "I think so. Come on."

Desi followed her sister downstairs into the den, where their parents kept their paperwork and personal files. The room looked in need of straightening, but their father had flatly refused his wife's pleas to redecorate. "This is my realm, Eva," he'd said. "I want someplace in my own house that feels like the inside of my bedroom slippers, not a page out of some decorator's magazine."

Their mother had consented, but usually kept the door closed. Once inside, Val started rummaging through the bookcase. "I noticed our baby books on the shelf ages ago. They were up near the top." She rose to her tiptoes. "Ah! Here they are."

She dragged them off in a clump, and sat down on the floor. Eagerly Desi sat beside her. Val blew dust off the tops. "There are three of them," she said quietly.

Desi's heart thudded. Sure enough, Val laid out three books on the beige carpet—two pink and a blue. Desi barely saw hers and Val's. Her attention zeroed in on the blue one. The girls glanced at each other. "I didn't know Mom kept one on the other baby." She felt acutely uncomfortable, as if she was looking at something forbidden.

"Me either." Val flipped it open. " 'Matthew Jeremy Mitchell,' " she read aloud. The ink had faded, making the name appear as ghostly as the child. The date of his birth had been recorded, along with his weight and length, but nothing else.

"It's a nice name. Do you remember him at all?" Desi asked.

Val concentrated hard. "All I remember is being afraid."

"Why?"

"Because—" Val ran her hand across her eyes, as if the memory was hurting her. "Because mom cried all the time. I was only two, you know, but I still remember her crying for days and days, and how scared I was because she wouldn't stop crying."

"And I didn't even exist," Desi observed.

"I do remember when *you* were born though." Val shoved aside the blue baby book and picked up Desi's.

"Did Mom and Dad hire a band?"

"No . . . In fact they were sort of quiet about it."

"Quiet?"

"I remember I was really excited—Aunt Clare too. I thought you were going to be my own personal baby doll. Little did I know that real babies cried a lot at night."

Val giggled, and Desi tried to act silly about it too, but it bothered her knowing that her parents hadn't been very enthusiastic about her arrival. "Of course that was so long ago," Val continued. "I was four when they brought you home from the hospital. You were tiny and wrinkled-looking . . . and you screamed most nights." She put her hands over her ears, and Desi almost felt that she should apologize for having kept her sister awake. "Aunt Clare called you 'colicky.' I remember the word because it was one of the first grown-up words I could pronounce. She used to visit, and we played with you."

"I'm surprised you remember."

"I just recall bits and pieces. Besides, by then I was the big girl, according to Aunt Clare, and you were the baby. I remember how Aunt Clare and I walked you in your stroller in the park."

On the inside Desi was a turmoil of emotions. It hurt realizing that her mother had ignored her as a baby and that Valerie actually *had* been the favorite all her life. At least Aunt Clare had always cared.

She leaned over to view her baby book, and with surprise saw that most of the pages were blank. "There's not much written in it," she mumbled, her hurt dissolving into embarrassment.

She picked up Val's. Every page was filled. Val's

first tooth. Val's first birthday. A silken lock of hair from Val's first haircut. With a nervous laugh Val shut the book. "Goodness, doesn't it just go to show you how busy Mom was by the time you came along."

How long could it take to jot down a few words, Desi thought. She said, "I guess so," and stared uncomfortably at the floor. "All the more reason to keep a book for Alicia," she added. "Someday she'll be glad that somebody cared enough to go to the trouble."

The door to the den swung open. "Val, I've been looking for you. Your wash is clean and—" The sentence died on their mother's lips as she took in the scene and spied the baby books spread out on the floor. "What are you two doing?" Her eyes narrowed, and both girls hurriedly grabbed for the three books.

"Taking a trip down memory lane," Val offered cheerfully, standing.

"Where did you find those?"

"On the bookshelves." Val motioned over her shoulder, stacked the books, and reached to put them away.

"Why did you want to see them?"

Desi saw that the color had left her mother's face, making Desi feel guilty of doing something wrong. "I bought Alicia a baby book," she began to explain. "We were just looking through ours to see how you kept them for us." She wondered if her mother remembered that hers was practically blank.

"Alicia! I swear, Desi, that's all I ever hear from you. Your life is totally taken over by that baby, and I don't like it one bit."

"No, it's not."

"Don't argue with me. Now you're spending your allowance on her. Just throwing it away."

"That's not so."

"I'm tired of discussing it." Her mother silenced Desi with a stern look and turned to Valerie. "I'd like you to come help me sort through your laundry. You might not want to take everything back to school, since you'll be home for Christmas in a few weeks. I'll be in your room." She didn't wait for Valerie to respond. She left the den with a firm jerk on the doorknob.

Valerie turned toward Desi, her expression stunned. "I can't remember ever seeing her so angry. Mom's *really* against your ChildCare work. Maybe you *had* better reconsider what you're doing, Desi."

Still feeling the sting of her mother's rebuke, Desi said nothing. Val quickly ran up to her room, leaving Desi to return the books to the shelves. Holding Alicia's baby book tightly, Desi kept seeing the stricken look on her mother's face. Something else was going on with her mother besides objections to Desi's volunteer work at ChildCare. Desi couldn't imagine what it was, but she was certain it was something very serious.

Chapter Twelve

"That's not the way you hang tinsel. You have to drape it carefully across each branch." Tamara demonstrated by placing a single strand of tinsel over the partially decorated tree standing in the ChildCare living room.

"We'll be here all night if we do it that way," Sadie fussed, but she followed Tamara's example.

Desi stood back and surveyed their handiwork. The giant spruce filled the bay window, and its fragrance mingled with those coming from the kitchen, where the volunteers and staff of ChildCare had gathered for a small Christmas party. "I think the tree looks fabulous," she announced.

Sadie harumphed, while Tamara rehung a clump of tinsel. "It's getting there," Tamara insisted.

"Are you all still fiddling with that tree?" Gayle asked, breezing into the room. "It'll be July before you get it finished at this pace," she joked. Dwayne groped for a glass ball, but Gayle held him back. "No way, buster."

Desi jiggled the infant walker at her feet, where Alicia sat. Desi stooped and rubbed noses with the baby. The infant craned her neck to see the tree. "You like that tree, darling?"

Alicia's tiny hand reached upward, as if to snare the glittering light beams. "There's a present under it just for you," Desi told her. Alicia kept her eyes on the tree, and Desi scooted across the rug and retrieved the silver foil box she'd wrapped the baby's red velvet dress in.

She held the box in front of the walker, and Alicia studied it for a moment, then tugged at the blue-and-silver bow. Desi laughed. "Not yet, sweetie. You have to wait until Christmas."

Tamara crouched next to her on the carpet. "What did you buy her?" Desi described the dress in great detail, and Tamara exclaimed, "Sounds gorgeous."

"There's room for her to grow too, so she should be able to wear it for quite some time." Because of the reading she was doing, Desi knew that Alicia was both underweight and small for her age, as were most HIV-positive babies.

"By next Christmas it'll be out of fashion and you'll buy her something new," Tamara kidded as she draped tinsel over her ears and shook her head to make it dance. Alicia laughed.

"I bought her a baby book too."

"That's a neat idea. Maybe I'll get one for Heather."

"I thought Gayle could help me fill in the blanks."

"What's Santa going to bring Desi for Christmas?" Tamara asked as she placed the gift back under the tree for Desi.

"Clothes, I guess. You know, the usual."

"Me too. At least I hope so. You're lucky that you don't have a bunch of sisters competing for Santa's bag."

"No, just Valerie," Desi said, but couldn't help thinking about Matthew Jeremy. What would she have given to a sixteen-year-old brother?

"Well I know one thing I wish Santa would give me for Christmas," Tamara continued. "I wish he'd give me a boyfriend."

She sounded so emphatic that Desi giggled. "Why?"

"Come on, girl! Don't tell me you wouldn't want someone special putting goodies into your Christmas stocking."

Still amused, Desi shook her head. "No way. I've got big plans for *my* life."

"You don't want to get married?"

"Not particularly."

"But I've seen you with Alicia. Don't tell me you don't want a baby!"

Desi didn't know how to answer her. In the months she'd been a volunteer at ChildCare, she'd felt things she'd never expected to feel. "All these babies are mine. And I didn't have to get married to have them."

Tamara rolled her eyes. "Talk about vicarious living!"

Both girls erupted into laughter. Alicia glanced from one to the other, squealing and waving her hands. Desi hugged her impulsively.

Gayle came over to where they were sitting. "What's making the three of you so happy?"

"Christmas cheer," Desi answered.

"Why don't you all come into the kitchen for a minute. We've just made some hot apple cider, and there's someone I want you to meet."

Desi hauled Alicia from the stroller, and cuddling her close, followed Tamara and Gayle into the brightly lit kitchen. People stood in clusters, drinking cider and munching decorated cookies. The sweet smells of sugar and cinnamon tickled Desi's nose.

"I want you to meet a friend of mine, Elizabeth Harris. She's a reporter for the *Atlanta Journal*." Gayle named the city's largest newspaper and motioned to an attractive young blond woman.

"Hi." Elizabeth shook both girls' hands and made a fuss over Alicia. "Gayle tells me you're both volunteers. I'd like to interview and photograph you for a feature story I'm doing for next Sunday's edition of the paper. Would you mind?"

Desi exchanged glances with Tamara. "I'd love it," Tamara said eagerly. Desi was hesitant as she considered her mother's possible reaction.

Gayle touched her shoulder. "Now I know I

fussed at you about bringing strangers into the house a few weeks ago, but Liz is no novice. She's been covering the medical scene in Atlanta for years."

"It's okay," Desi started, realizing Gayle couldn't possibly know her true reason for vacillating.

"It's just that we depend so much on community support," Gayle continued earnestly. "It goes beyond caring for the babies. We have to maintain the house and the grounds, as well as look to the future. One day we'll need playground equipment for these kids."

"Since Christmas is the perfect time for giving—" Elizabeth added with a happy shrug, "Gayle thought a feature story would help bring in more money and helpers. But reporters always look for a good angle, and I think a feature on you two—on kids helping babies—would be a terrific approach. What do you say?"

If it would help ChildCare and Alicia, Desi knew she couldn't refuse. Besides, Tamara was practically bursting to be interviewed. "Good," the attractive reporter said when both girls nodded. "While I'm interviewing you, Dave here will take some photos."

Stuffing the remains of a cookie in his mouth, the photographer began snapping photos. For the next twenty minutes Desi and Tamara answered dozens of questions, and by the time they were through,

Alicia had fallen fast asleep on Desi's shoulder. "I guess I need to get her to bed," she told Elizabeth.

"I guess you do," Elizabeth said as Dave took one final photo.

Gently Desi carried the sleeping baby into her bedroom, laid her down, and covered her with her favorite flannel blanket. A night light glowed from the wall, thrusting shadows away from the crib with its pale yellow hue.

Alicia's eyelids fluttered open, and when the baby saw Desi's face, they swept downward and closed in peaceful sleep. Desi caressed the soft cheek lovingly and tiptoed from the room with the sweet scent of baby's breath clinging to her heart.

"Can I eat lunch with you?" Corrine asked above the noise in the school cafeteria.

Desi stopped chewing and glanced up from the book she was reading, surprised. "Suit yourself," she said, and went back to her book.

"I saw the article in the newspaper. It was pretty interesting."

"Thanks." She continued to chew without looking up. Actually she'd known she'd been a topic of conversation in the halls all morning.

"Some of my friends told me they thought it was pretty awesome. Not just the article, but the volunteering bit too." Corrine toyed with the food on her plate as she spoke.

"I think that the reporter did a good job of explaining about the babies," Desi said, skimming a page in her book without really reading the words. "Especially about what's probably ahead for them if they contract AIDS."

"Yes. The story sure was informative."

Desi finally looked up at Corrine. "Do you want something special?"

Her old friend reddened. "I've been sort of missing you, that's all." Desi arched an eyebrow, but didn't respond. "I haven't been much of a friend lately. I admit I was put off by your volunteer work. That and the fact that my mother had an anxiety attack when she heard you worked with AIDS babies. She didn't want me hanging around with you."

"You could have said something to me and been honest instead of ignoring me. Our friendship should have counted for *something*."

"You're right. I should have." Corrine looked miserable, and Desi's iciness toward her was almost thawing. "I'm really sorry, Desi. I should have been a better friend, and I was hoping we could still be friends."

"What about Randy, the love of your life?" Desi wasn't sure she was ready to completely forgive Corrine.

"We're history."

All around them the lunchroom clattered with the sounds of trays and silverware, of talking and laughter, but between them there was silence. Desi broke it. "I'm still working with Alicia. Nothing's changed in that way."

"The baby in the article—yes. Alicia's pretty cute."

"So I still won't have the Good Housekeeping Seal of Approval for your mother's benefit. How's she going to react if we start hanging around together again?"

"Mom read the article too, and I think she understands better." Desi wished her own mother understood better. When she'd read the article, all she'd done was moan about how everybody in town would know about her daughter's association with AIDS. It really hurt knowing that her mother cared more about what people thought than about Desi's feelings. Her dad had acted better—even proud of her. Brian had been great. The moment she'd come into biology class that morning, he'd smiled and given her a thumb's-up signal.

Corrine asked, "What do you say? Can we be friends again?"

"What about all your new friends? I know they're important to you."

Corrine nodded. "Yes, they are. But can't I have both?"

The question sounded sincere, and Desi realized that both she and Corrine had changed over the past few months. Had she been insensitive to Corrine all this time? So caught up in her own interests that she had ignored her longtime friend's needs? If they were truly friends, then couldn't their friendship survive their each having other interests?

"Yes, you can," Desi said slowly. "In fact I think it's a good idea for both of us. I'm sorry that I got so involved in ChildCare that I forgot about other things."

Corrine looked relieved and flashed a smile. "I really do have a ton of stuff to tell you. I've missed our talks."

"I've missed them too. Call me. I'll be home tonight after ten."

When the bell rang, Desi watched Corrine hurry away. She knew they had a lot of work to do in order to feel close to each other again, but she felt better about their friendship than she had in a long, long time.

That afternoon, when Desi arrived at Child-Care, Gayle was waiting for her. "We need to talk," Gayle told her.

"What's wrong? Is Alicia sick?"

"She's fine."

"Is it Anthony?"

"Actually Anthony's doing much better."

Desi felt a quick moment of gratitude. "That's good." She asked, "Did I do something wrong again?"

Gayle shook her head. "It's nothing like that." She took a deep breath. "It's just that the human resources department called me this morning to say that Alicia's mother has asked to see her daughter."

Chapter Thirteen

❧

Desi went cold all over. "What do you mean?"

"Ever since Alicia's birth, her mother has been in drug rehab. She's been living in a halfway house here in Atlanta. It seems she's been drug-free for the past six months. She never signed away her rights to her baby, and now she's asked to meet with her."

"But she has no right—"

Gayle squeezed Desi's shoulder. "Honey, she has every right. She's the baby's mother."

"But she hasn't done anything for Alicia since she was born! She deserted her."

"She was hooked on cocaine. She couldn't do anything for Alicia."

"Now she can just come back and say she's fine and take Alicia away?" Desi felt sick to her stomach.

"You know that's not the way we do things. For starters, she can't simply say she's fine and get her baby back. She must prove it. Remember, I told you at the beginning that the human resources people carefully supervise all visits. A social worker will bring Alicia to an arranged location, where she will allow the mother an hour alone with her baby."

Desi fidgeted with a sofa pillow while Gayle

talked. "Also, there would be many such visits over a course of time before the baby could return to the mother. Even if the mother is allowed to keep the baby, there would be follow-up visits and close monitoring of the situation."

Gayle lifted Desi's chin with her forefinger. "We all want what's best for the baby, don't we? And Alicia does, after all, have a mother."

"If her mother takes her back, where will she live?" Desi could hardly get the question out.

"In the halfway house, for the time being. Then, whenever Alicia's mother gets on her feet, gets a job and all—well, anywhere she wants to live."

"When is the meeting?" Desi hoped her question sounded casual and not as panicked as she felt.

"This coming Saturday. I'll drive Alicia downtown, where the social worker assigned to her mother will pick her up and take her over to the halfway house. If it's a sunny day, there's a park across the street, and that's where the meeting will take place. Otherwise it will be at the human resources offices."

"Will she be alone with her?"

"For a little while," Gayle said. "About an hour. I'll take a stroller too. That way her mother can walk her around the park. Afterward the social worker will bring Alicia back downtown, and I'll bring her back here."

"What time is the meeting?"

"Noon." Gayle paused. "Don't worry, we'll have her home by supper."

"I want to dress her for the meeting," Desi blurted out. "I want her mother to see what good care we're giving her. Maybe if she does, she'll realize that she can't take care of her half as well. After all, she's got HIV, and she was an addict."

Gayle started to say something, but patted Desi's shoulder instead. "Look, if you want to dress Alicia to meet with her mother, it's fine with me. Please pack a diaper bag to take too, okay?"

Desi headed for the playroom, but stopped at the doorway and asked, "What's her name anyway?"

"Who's?"

"Alicia's mother's."

"Sherrie Rowe."

Desi told her, "Thanks for letting me know," and stepped through the doorway.

The morning of the trip, when Tamara tried to help prepare Alicia, Desi shooed her away. "I want to do this by myself," she told her friend.

First Desi bathed the baby, letting her splash the way she loved. Alicia poked her yellow rubber duck beneath the water, then laughed gleefully when it popped to the surface. Next Desi dried her carefully, playing peekaboo for a few minutes before placing her on the changing table. She sprinkled baby power and rubbed sweet-smelling baby lotion on Alicia's tummy.

"You don't have to be on your very best behavior, you know," Desi advised the infant. "It's all right to pitch a fit. Your mother needs to see that just because you look like an angel, you don't always act like one." Alicia's bright eyes followed her as Desi worked the tiny legs into pale pink tights. "And if you spit up, be sure it's on her and not your outfit." Alicia gurgled and reached for the necklace that dangled from Desi's neck.

Desi pulled a shirt over Alicia's head, then slipped on a dress and a white sweater. She picked up a soft baby hairbrush and pulled it through the head of tight, black curls, clipped a large fuchsia bow into the hair, and slipped shiny black patent leather shoes onto Alicia's tiny feet.

"She's adorable," Tamara said as she came into the room carrying Dwayne.

It was true—the baby looked so beautiful that a lump rose in Desi's throat. "I better put her parka on her, don't you think? The weatherman said it wasn't going to be warmer than fifty-five today."

"The sun's shining nice and bright," Tamara said, looking through the nursery window. "It'll probably be warmer out in the sun."

Desi sat the baby in her crib with a few toys and set about filling a diaper bag with fresh diapers, Alicia's rubber duck, a teddy bear, and a few teething toys. "Maybe I should write a note saying she's cutting her back teeth and may need this gel rubbed on them." She held up a tube of ointment.

Tamara shook her head. "It'll be all right."

"Well, if her gums hurt, she'll start crying."

"Desi, it'll be okay," Tamara repeated.

"I know," Desi said with a helpless shrug. "It's just hard, that's all. I never once thought that her mother would ever ask to see her. I sort of forgot that she even had a mother."

"Well, Sadie told me that Heather's mother set up three appointments to meet with Heather and the social worker, and she didn't show up for one meeting."

"She didn't?"

"Nope. And after the third time they never heard from her again. Heather's a ward of the state, and her mother won't ever get her back."

Desi hung the diaper bag over her shoulder, lifted Alicia from the crib, and carried her into the kitchen. Tamara followed.

"My, my, doesn't she look the picture of a princess," Sadie said as she looked up from loading the dishwasher. "You've done a fine job of fixing her up to see her mama."

Desi sat in the rocker, turned Alicia to face her, and proceeded to put the parka on her. Midway through the process Gayle sailed into the kitchen.

"Oh, Desi, she looks lovely. Thanks for dressing her so nicely. Would you mind buckling her into her car seat for me while I get the stroller?"

"No problem," Desi said, carrying Alicia out to the car.

Tenderly she sat Alicia in the infant seat and buckled the straps. Gayle came out, unlocked the trunk, and slid the stroller inside. "Now, don't you worry," Gayle said. "She'll be home by late afternoon."

Together they stood next to the car. "It's all arranged with the social worker," Gayle said. "I understand Alicia's mother is really looking forward to this."

Desi offered a tight smile. "I hope it goes well."

Gayle opened the car door and got behind the wheel. "I'm proud of you, Desi. You're handling this very well, and I appreciate your attitude. I know how much Alicia means to you."

"What's the big deal?" Desi said with a shrug. "It's just a little visit. Maybe she won't even show up."

"You can't tell," Gayle called cheerily, over the sound of the engine. Desi waved and watched the car wind up the drive to the brick gateway, where it turned onto the road. Sunlight glanced off the metal, and a cool breeze stirred up the leaves at her feet. As soon as the vehicle had disappeared, Desi hurried indoors, her heart pounding. Fortunately the kitchen was empty.

She fumbled in her jeans pocket for a scrap of paper, picked up the phone, and punched in the written numbers. She heard one ring, and when the receiver on the other end was lifted, she didn't wait for a greeting, but said breathlessly, "They just left. I'll be waiting for you right at the end of the driveway. And hurry, Brian. We have to beat them downtown."

Chapter Fourteen

~⟞⟍⟋~

"Honestly Desi, doing this makes me feel sneaky. First I have to wait by that pay phone at the corner gas station, then you call, and I rush over and pick you up. And now we're trying to break a speed record into downtown. What am I—a detective?" Brian wove his car in and out of freeway traffic as he grumbled.

"You said you'd help me. We've got to get downtown before Gayle hands over the baby so we can see the social worker's car and follow her to the park. Can you go any faster?"

"Don't worry, we'll get there. I don't know how I ever let you talk me into this."

Sitting in Brian's car and speeding down the expressway was making Desi wonder the same thing. How had she ever decided to spy on the meeting between Alicia and her mother? Where had she gotten the courage to call Brian the night before and work out the details of such a scheme?

She had outlined the plan over the phone, and he'd listened in silence. "Will you do it?" she had asked in a voice full of emotion.

"Why can't you ask Gayle if you could tag along?"

Desi had squeezed the receiver in frustration. "Are you serious? She's not going to take *me* to meet Alicia's mother."

"Why the cloak-and-dagger routine? Why can't I just pick you up at the ChildCare house as soon as they leave?"

"Think about it—Sadie's seen your car, and she'll ask questions. She might even say something to Gayle, and I promised Gayle I wouldn't have you visit again—"

"Calm down," he'd said. "So you got the number of the pay phone at the gas station?"

"I walked over and wrote it down this afternoon. You have to be waiting at ten-thirty on the dot, because Gayle's driving Alicia downtown for the hook-up with the social worker."

He'd gone silent, and Desi had felt her heart pounding. "I need your help, Brian."

She'd heard him release a deep breath. "All right. I'll do it, but I don't think it's such a good idea."

Now, weaving in and out of traffic, Desi herself was thinking it hadn't been such a bright idea, but she'd come too far to turn back. "Slow down!" she cried, pointing. "There's Gayle's car. I guess that's the social worker she's talking with." Gayle had pulled alongside another car in downtown Atlanta and was speaking to the driver.

"Give our junior spy a merit badge," Brian muttered, slowing his car and causing the driver behind him to lean on his horn.

Desi ducked, in case Gayle should look over at the commotion. Brian started a running commentary. "Subject A is carrying Baby Girl Subject to a red Mazda and strapping her in. Now Subject A is getting into her car and starting the engine. She's heading west toward the freeway. Baby Girl Subject does not seem to be crying."

"Oh, knock it off," Desi growled, scooting up to where she could peer over the dashboard. She saw the back of a red car a few car lengths in front of them. "Don't let them get too far ahead," she commanded.

"Who's leading this escapade, ace? My faithful chariot can keep up."

Desi straightened in the seat and riveted her gaze on the social worker's car. Thirty minutes later they turned onto a side street that wound through a suburb. The social worker pulled her car into a parking area adjoining a park. Brian chose a space some rows over as Desi watched the social worker unload the stroller and put Alicia in it. Desi tugged on Brian's arm as the woman started pushing Alicia toward a cluster of park benches. "Come on."

"Why do you still need me? I'd feel better waiting here."

"I don't want to look suspicious."

"I guess some girl peeking from behind trees

would be pretty weird." He opened his car door. "Come on, Sherlock. Let's go."

They headed in the direction of the benches. In the distance Desi saw the social worker talking to a girl. At first she thought that the social worker was asking directions, but soon she saw her lift Alicia out of the stroller and hand her over to the girl. Desi stared. "Do you suppose that's *her*?"

Brian gazed surreptitiously in every direction. "It's a good bet."

The social worker handed the girl the diaper bag and walked away. The girl sat down on the bench with Alicia and patted the baby awkwardly. "If that's Alicia's mother, she's just a kid!" Desi exclaimed. "I need to get closer." She dragged him forward.

When they were about ten yards away, Desi stopped and studied the girl, taking care to remain well out of the angle of Alicia's vision. Desi thought that the girl's jeans and jeans jacket looked brand-new. Obviously she had dressed for the occasion. The girl held the baby gingerly, as if Alicia were a bomb that might go off. Alicia appeared bewildered, and her lower lip quivered as if she were deciding whether or not to cry. Desi had the urge to run up and take the baby away.

"Alicia's mother is so young," Desi whispered, dismayed.

"What did you expect? Some woman with two other kids and a briefcase?"

"Of course not. I just didn't think she'd be our age."

The girl unzipped Alicia's parka and examined her clothing. "She shouldn't do that," Desi said. "Alicia could catch a cold."

"Give it up, Desi. We don't belong here." Brian took her securely by the arm and pulled her back toward the parking lot.

"What are you doing?"

"Getting us out of here."

"Let me go."

"You're coming with me." At the car he opened the door and pushed her inside.

"I don't want to leave!"

Brian got in and slammed the door hard. "We're leaving."

"I'm not leaving!" She pulled on the door handle. It fell off in her hand. "Oh, great. This piece of junk—"

Brian took the metal handle and tossed it into the backseat. "I can fix it. Now listen to me. Look at me when I'm talking to you." Reluctantly she allowed her eyes to meet his. "You are *not* Alicia's mother. That girl *is*—and she deserves to spend some time alone with her kid without having you hanging out of the bushes spying on her."

For a moment Desi wanted to murder Brian, but suddenly tears brimmed in her eyes. She sniffed and looked away. He was right, of course. Alicia didn't belong to her. Not really. "Aw, come on," he said, turning on the engine and putting the car into reverse. "I know this isn't easy for you. How about if I buy you some pizza?"

"Do you solve every crisis with food?" she snapped.

They didn't speak again until they were sitting inside a pizza parlor and Brian had ordered for them. At last he broke the silence. "I'm sorry I was rough on you." She didn't respond. "It's just that you're making too big a deal out of this thing. You're setting yourself up to get hurt."

Desi sat on her hands. "I don't want to lose her."

"You won't."

She felt defeated and miserable. "I suppose you think I'm an idiot. Why should some girl like me care about some poor baby who may contract a terrible, incurable disease—a baby whose own mother walked out on her as soon as she was born?" Desi fought back tears. "Maybe that's why I *do* care. I mean, what kind of mother doesn't want her own daughter?" Deep down Desi realized how much she could relate to the feeling of being unwanted, but she couldn't say that to Brian.

"Don't judge Alicia's mother like that. You don't know why she gave her up, and you don't know what her life's like."

Desi resented him for pointing out her judgmental attitude. What did he know about mothers' love for their daughters? She felt miserable and began to cry.

Brian came around to her side of the booth, slid in beside her, and put his arm around her shoulder. She buried her face in his neck and cried harder. She groped for a napkin, and he handed her several. "You feel better now?" he asked.

The cry had been therapeutic. She *did* feel better. She blew her nose. "My eyes are all red and puffy, aren't they?"

"You look fine. Like a girl who *cares.*" He stroked her hair, and she rested her head on his shoulder. "I can't answer your questions, Desi. I don't know why the world's the way it is. I don't know why some people get handed life on a silver platter and others get paper plates with grease spots."

His voice rumbled in her ear. "What good does it do to ask why anyway? What's important is that we make the best of what we do get. You can't change what's happened to Alicia, but you care about her. You've given her a whole lot more than she'd ever have gotten if you hadn't been in her life. I'll bet, if you think about it, she's given you a whole lot back in the same way."

Desi agreed—what Brian said was true. How empty her life would be if it weren't for Alicia. And the others at ChildCare too. She'd never have met Tamara or Gayle or any of the babies. She'd never have felt so needed or so capable of giving something of herself. "I guess you're right."

Just then the waitress brought the pizza. "Now eat up, and I'll take you wherever you want to go," Brian said as he served her a slice.

"In your chariot?" Her voice sounded husky. "I'm sorry I called it a piece of junk."

"You're forgiven."

After they ate, Brian took her to a mall, where they window-shopped and where she bought Alicia a stuffed toy. It was dark when he took her to Child-Care and parked on the street outside the brick entrance. He shut off his engine, but didn't make a move to get out. "You okay?"

"I'm okay."

"So what're you going to do over Christmas break?"

In the turmoil of the past few days, she'd forgotten that school was officially out until after New Year's. "My sister's home. I guess we'll just hang around. I'm planning on doubling up on my hours here at ChildCare. How about you?"

"Mom's dragging me and my sister down to Florida to visit our grandparents."

Desi felt a twinge of disappointment. "So I guess this is it until next year."

In the light from the street lamp, she saw him smile at her little joke. "Guess so. You sure you don't want me to drive you home right now?"

"No. I want to get Alicia ready for bed. Besides,

my aunt's here tonight, so she'll take me home." She reached for the handle, but of course it was gone.

Brian hopped out of the car and came around for her. The air felt chilly as they stood beside the car. "I appreciate your taking the time to run around with me today," she told him. "Even if it was a dumb idea."

"Hey, we're partners, right?"

"You had some good things to say too. I'll remember them." She peered up at him. "How'd you get so smart anyway?"

Moonlight spilled across his face. His expression looked solemn. "Some lessons you learn the hard way."

His response puzzled her, and she wanted to ask what he meant, but he pointed her down the driveway and gave her a gentle shove. "Now go on, before a cop pulls up and gives me a ticket for illegal parking."

She headed toward the house, but when she heard his door slam, she turned and called, "Have a Merry Christmas."

He started the car. "You too. And don't forget to have some *fun* over the holidays."

She watched him drive away and felt strangely alone. Brian was really very nice. There was something about him, something more than his good looks and easy camaraderie that touched her. Why, she was halfway looking forward to school's starting up, just so she could see him again.

The notion made her smile. Wouldn't he have a good laugh if he knew? Overhead, stars glowed in the cold, brittle air. Desi shivered, then hurried up the path, toward the cozily lit house, feeling light, almost buoyant. Her boots kicked up dry leaves and sent them scattering into the darkness.

Chapter Fifteen

As Christmas holidays went at her house, Desi thought, these were pretty good. She liked the presents she received, and her family seemed to like the ones she gave them. Aunt Clare came for Christmas dinner, and the conversation at the table didn't become strained, as it had at Thanksgiving.

Her father asked about her science project and almost sounded disappointed when she told him that she wasn't doing one this year. "My lab partner and I can't agree on a topic," Desi explained. "I'd like to do something about AIDS, and Brian doesn't want to do anything."

"But you've always entered," her father said. "And you've always done pretty well. Can't you enter on your own?"

"I'm busier this year," she told him, then cut her eyes toward her mother. She held her breath, waiting for a remark about how she was spending too much time at "that place," but fortunately her mother kept silent. "I'm still making good grades though."

"You're a smart girl," Aunt Clare interjected with a bright smile.

Later that afternoon Valerie drove Desi over to ChildCare. She pulled up outside the kitchen door in the small parking area alongside the car Desi knew was Sadie's. "Wish I could come in sometime," Val told her.

"I wish you could too," Desi agreed. "But I told you how strict they are about strangers. Gayle only invites people in under special conditions."

"I understand, but I'm just wondering if I'll ever see this Alicia in anything but photographs."

"I can hold her up to the window if you want to wait a few minutes," Desi said in a flash of inspiration.

"Sorry—but I can't today. I've scheduled a tennis match for this afternoon. If I'm smart enough to find my way to the playing court, that is."

The sarcasm in Val's voice made Desi pause. "Did what Aunt Clare say bother you?"

Val puffed warm air into her hands. "Maybe a little bit. It's no secret that you're the 'smart one'— and Aunt Clare's favorite."

And you're Mom's favorite, Desi wanted to tell her. "Haven't you always felt like there's some sort of sister rivalry thing going on between Mom and Aunt Clare?" Desi asked instead.

"I never thought much about it."

"Maybe it's because Aunt Clare never had her own family, but seems happier than Mom."

Val shrugged. "Maybe. It's Christmas. Let's not get into any heavy topics."

"Are things going better at school?"

"About the same," Val said with a sigh. "I can't believe I've got to face midterms when I get back. Then the collegiate tennis circuit starts in February, and my coach has been pretty vocal about us having a shot at regional playoffs this year."

"You'll do fine."

Val chewed on her bottom lip. "First I've got to get a decent grade point, or I won't play at all."

"You'll do fine, Val."

"I *have* to, don't I? I can't disappoint Mom or Coach."

Desi pulled on the door handle. "I should go. I want to see how Alicia looks in the dress I bought her."

"Take a picture so I can see too," Val called as Desi scooted out of the car.

Hurrying into the house, Desi entered the warm, cozy kitchen. "How's it going, Sadie? Did you have a good Christmas?"

Sadie was picking up toys and putting them into the playpen, where Anthony was just as busily tossing them out again. "Things are going fine, and yes, I had a good Christmas. I see you couldn't stay away either."

"Not on Christmas Day. I have to see Alicia." She patted Anthony's head. "He acts like he's never been sick a day. Hard to believe we almost lost him last month." Desi glanced around. "Where is Alicia anyway?"

"She's asleep."

"It's not nap time."

Sadie stooped down to retrieve a toy fire truck. "She woke up with the sniffles and isn't feeling too good."

"I'll check on her." Desi walked quickly through the living room, where piles of torn Christmas paper, boxes, and ribbons were stacked in one corner, and clusters of toys and clothing were strewn beneath the branches of the Christmas tree. Dried needles and limp tinsel littered the carpet.

In the bedroom Desi went straight to Alicia's crib. The baby lay under her flannel blanket. She was asleep, but her breathing sounded shallow. Desi's heart thudded as she reached down and touched Alicia's cheek. It felt fiery hot. At her touch Alicia woke, saw Desi, whimpered, and reached her arms upward.

Heart pounding, Desi scooped her up and hugged her tight. Her small body was so warm that Desi could feel the heat searing through the sleeper and blanket. Alicia coughed. "Poor baby," Desi whispered. "My poor, sweet little baby."

Clutching Alicia close, Desi hurried toward the kitchen to find Sadie.

"Exactly how sick is she?" Desi asked her aunt as they stood beside the crib in the Pediatric ICU.

"It's bronchitis," Aunt Clare said, her arm

around Desi's waist. "It's serious, but she'll be getting the very best treatment possible."

Once the ChildCare staff had decided Alicia
was too sick to remain at the house, she'd been taken
to County Hospital, where a pediatrician had
promptly admitted her and Desi had called Aunt
Clare. Alicia had been placed on a regime of IV
fluids and antibiotics, and now all they could do was
wait for the medicine to work. Desi gazed down at
the infant, shivering within a plastic tent over the
stainless steel crib. "I can hardly stand to look at
her," she confessed to her aunt. "She looks so small
and helpless inside that thing."

"It helps her breathe more easily."

"Do they *have* to tie her arm down?"

"She'd pull out her IVs if they didn't. Believe
me, honey, everything's being done with her welfare
in mind."

"Her eyes keep following me. She looks scared,
and when she looks at me, I know she wants me to
hold her." Desi stopped because her voice kept
catching.

"You can hold her when she gets better."

"She *will* get better, won't she? Please tell me
she's going to be all right. You know she's not like
other babies." The mechanical beeping and humming of the monitors droned in the dimly lit room.
Outside, it was evening, but in the enclosed room
Desi had no sense of time. "Anthony got better," she
said, half to encourage herself.

"Yes, he did." Aunt Clare took Desi's hand and led her toward the door. "It's late. Let me take you home."

"I don't want to leave her."

"Honey, it's Christmas Day. You should go home. You can return tomorrow. Your mother's worried—"

"I don't care what Mom says," Desi hissed. "I'm not abandoning Alicia."

"No one's asked you to. I just think you should go home and get some rest. Tomorrow's another day. Gayle's been called, and she'll be organizing volunteers—"

"Alicia knows me best. I plan to spend every minute I can with her," Desi insisted.

"She could be here quite a while. Please don't put yourself under that kind of pressure. Once school starts again—"

"How can I think about school? I'll skip school. I'm making straight A's."

"You can't skip months of school if she takes that long to recuperate," Aunt Clare replied. "I'll keep a close watch on her and keep you informed about her condition."

Once in the hallway, Desi braced herself against the wall and started to cry.

"I'm sure she'll be all right," her aunt said, but Desi brushed her aside.

"You don't know that," Desi whispered, rubbing the back of her hand across her eyes. "She could get sicker."

Aunt Clare shook her head in resignation. "We can only treat one complication at a time. Don't borrow trouble."

Feeling suddenly bone weary, Desi nodded and followed her aunt meekly down the hall to the elevators. In the lobby a skeleton staff manned the desk, Christmas decorations hung on walls, and white lights glittered from a single tree that stood like a weary sentinel. Desi rode in her aunt's car in silence, staring out into the black, cold night, while Christmas music played on the radio, reminding her that angels were bending down to touch golden harps. Quietly she prayed for one to touch Alicia and make her well.

Desi spent all of Christmas break going back and forth to the hospital. Either her aunt picked her up on her way to work or Valerie took her during the day. Surprisingly, the only thing her mother said about Desi's schedule was, "Are you sure you want to spend your entire break this way?"

"I'm sure," she answered in a tone of voice that all but dared her mother to tell her otherwise.

When her mother didn't challenge her, Desi felt relieved, but puzzled. She couldn't understand her mom's change of attitude. Once, Desi thought she'd seen tears in her mother's eyes, but she dismissed it as simply a trick of the light.

One afternoon Val came with Desi on her visit. "She looks so pitiful," Val said as they stood together next to Alicia's crib. "Too bad the first time I ever see her is under these conditions."

Desi reached under the plastic tent and stroked Alicia lovingly. "Gayle told me that her doctors are concerned because she's not responding to treatment."

"You're really worried, aren't you?"

"Yes." Desi's voice was barely a whisper.

"I'm sorry I have to go back to school and leave you to get through this by yourself. I thought that Mom and Dad might have been different now that Alicia's sick. I can't believe they never even want to talk to you about it."

"Dad's busy with work, but I think he cares in his way. I've learned not to expect him to get overly involved with much of anything. His attitude doesn't bother me so much." Desi shrugged. "But Mom's hated the whole idea from the first. She's a smart person, but she's still nervous about AIDS, and no matter how many times Aunt Clare and I tell her I won't catch the virus from Alicia, she won't believe us."

"You could really use Mom's support," Val acknowledged, patting Desi's shoulder.

"I have Aunt Clare and all the people from ChildCare. Tamara's dad too. He's a minister." Desi turned toward her sister. "You've been great also, Val. Thanks a lot."

"You'll call me if something changes?"

Desi promised she would.

On New Year's Day Val loaded her luggage back into her roommate's car and left for college. The next day Desi returned to Grady. She told Brian what was happening, and at lunch she also told Corrine. Both were sympathetic, and their concern about her—as well as Alicia—was heartening.

After dinner Desi was dialing Aunt Clare's number from the kitchen phone when her mother came up to her. "Don't call your aunt," she said. "I'll drive you to the hospital. I won't go up to see the baby, but I would like to take you."

Afraid to risk losing her mother's offer by asking questions, Desi grabbed her coat and dashed out the door. They drove in strained silence, and when they got there, her mother said, "Call me when you want to come home."

Desi told her thanks and hurried inside the hospital. As she got off the elevator, she saw Gayle talking to Alicia's physician. "Alicia's been moved into isolation," Gayle said, when Desi approached.

"Why?"

"Pneumonia."

Desi caught her breath. "That's much worse than bronchitis."

"Yes, it is. Specifically, it's *Pneumocystis carinii*," the physician explained.

Desi felt as if all the oxygen had been sucked from her. Alicia had developed the type of pneumonia most associated with AIDS. No one had to spell out what the diagnosis meant. Only a miracle could save baby Alicia now.

Chapter Sixteen

Desi absolutely refused to go to school the next day. "I'm going to the hospital," she told her mother defiantly. "You can make me go to school, but I'll skip and go to the hospital. Alicia's dying." Just saying the word made her sick to her stomach, but her aunt had been brutally honest with her the night before. There was little medical science could do for Alicia at this point except ease her suffering.

"You can't let your entire life revolve around this child," her mother insisted from the doorway of Desi's bedroom.

Desi slammed her bureau drawer. "And why can't I?"

"It isn't healthy."

"Look who's talking!" Desi exclaimed, not caring how her mother reacted. "That never stopped *you* from hanging all over Valerie's life. From turning her into your 'perfect' clone."

"What are you talking about?" Her mother looked shocked. "What's your cutting school got to do with Valerie?"

Desi was instantly sorry she'd brought up her sister and her long unspoken feelings about her mother's attitudes. She threw up her hands in frustration. "You don't understand anything! You don't understand me and maybe not Valerie either. You don't care about anything outside these four walls! Alicia's going to die, Mom. Doesn't it bother you at all?"

"What's all the shouting about?" Desi's father asked, coming down the hall, still knotting his tie.

"Desi's refusing to go to school. She's insisting on going to the hospital instead."

Her mother had ignored Desi's plea for Alicia. Desi ran to her father. "Make her understand, Daddy. Alicia's so sick. I just have to be with her."

"Maybe a couple of days won't hurt, Eva."

"Not you too? This baby is *dying.*"

"Babies die, Eva" his voice grew solemn. "We both know that, don't we? There's not much we can do about it. I think Desi needs to go." His look was inscrutable, but Desi saw her mother's expression go stony. Without another word her mother walked away.

"That's right," Desi's father called after her. "Go ahead and pretend it isn't happening. Just shut your eyes and walk off! That's the way to handle the problem. Pretending won't make it go away, you know."

Desi felt confused and fearful. What was going on between her parents? "Dad?" Agitated, he turned back toward her. "Can I go to the hospital?"

"It's all right for the next day or so, but you'll

have to work it around your school schedule after that. You can't stay away however long it takes until . . ." He didn't finish his sentence, but rubbed the back of his neck wearily. "Will your aunt be there?" he finally asked.

"Someone from ChildCare is always there. Sometimes it's Aunt Clare."

"Then get your things. I'll drop you off."

She grabbed her purse and followed him out the door.

It was almost four o'clock the next afternoon when Brian found her in the ICU waiting room. "You're missing classes, and Mr. Redding isn't feeling too sympathetic." He leaned against the doorjamb, his arms crossed over his chest.

"I don't care about biology. I don't care about anything but Alicia."

Brian shifted. "He said that if we did a special project, we could get extra points and that would make up for your absences."

"Didn't you hear me? *I don't care.*"

"Maybe I do."

His sudden interest in a biology project made her angry. "When I wanted to do a project, you backed out. Now you suddenly want to do one because our grade is taking a nosedive. What gives with you?" Before he could answer, she added, "If we did anything, it would have to be about AIDS. I don't have the time to research anything else right now. Take it or leave it."

He rotated his massive shoulders as if to release tension. "Desi, I want to explain about what I told you—or *didn't* tell you, actually—about doing a project on AIDS."

"I'm not in the mood." She knew she was acting testy, but didn't care.

Brian looked up and down the corridor, at the nurses' station and the activity. "Is there someplace we can talk in private?"

"Talk about what?"

"I want to tell you something really personal."

She was hesitant to leave, but he looked so determined, she couldn't tell him no. "There's a chapel downstairs."

They went down in the elevator to a room where a stained-glass window cast blue light over a few wooden pews. They were alone in the tiny interfaith chapel.

"Do you come here much?" Brian asked.

"Just when I want to take a break, or whenever I need to get myself together." They walked to the front and sat in a pew that faced a painting of sparrows flitting through green trees. For some reason the tiny birds reminded her of Alicia. "You said you wanted to tell me something. I don't want to be away from Alicia for too long, so if you could just tell me . . ."

He hunched forward, resting his forearms on

his knees. "I wanted to tell you why I didn't want to do a project on AIDS."

"It's not important now."

"I wanted to tell you that day at the park, after you found the message on your locker."

She turned sideways in the pew, facing him, feeling impatient, wishing she were back upstairs. "You always act understanding and never seem to mind that I volunteer at ChildCare. I never thought the subject of AIDS bothers you."

"Oh, it bothers me all right."

"Since when?"

"Ever since my uncle died from it, two years ago." Brian was staring down at his hands.

"Why didn't you tell me? I would have understood."

"Would you? My uncle was gay. He loved men. He caught AIDS from having unprotected sex, and he died."

Despite everything she knew about AIDS, his news upset her. Partly because she could see how painful it was for Brian to discuss it. "You should have said something. I thought we were friends."

"How could I? I've had a hard time accepting it myself. Not only because he was homosexual, but because he died."

"Were you close to your uncle?"

"Yes."

"I still don't understand about the biology proj-

ect. If you know all about AIDS, then why didn't
you want to work on a project about it?"

He shrugged, causing the blue sunbeams to
creep farther down his back. "Doing the project
would only have reminded me of how badly I
treated him."

"How so?"

"When we first found out about Uncle Mark's
AIDS, I was thirteen. Man, I torqued out. He was
like a father to me—my hero." The phrase sounded
sarcastic. "He was thirty, good-looking, had a good
job. And he played basketball with me, and rack-
etball, and took me camping—did all the things my
father never did because he lived so far away. I
thought Uncle Mark was the greatest man alive.

"Mom was his sister, and the night he told us
about being sick, I lost it. I called him a bunch of
names and ran off. I know I hurt him—I meant to."

"Didn't you ever tell him you were sorry?"

"No. I wrote him off. Mom tried to help me
understand, but I tuned her out. He moved to New
York City so as not to be a bother to us. Mom kept in
touch. Eventually he ended up in an AIDS hospice
up there. He wrote me, but I tore up his letters. All I
could think was 'What if my friends find out?' The
whole time he was sick I never contacted him. I took
the job in the health club so I could stay busy and
not have to think about him."

"You told me it helped you blow off steam."

He laughed mirthlessly. "Yeah. I blew off a lot

of it over the two years he was sick. I felt like he'd betrayed me—lied to me about who and what he was. In the end he contracted pneumonia, went down to ninety pounds, and couldn't swallow. He died at the hospice with no family around him. I'll never forget the day they called and told us. Mom was a mess. She flew up for his funeral, but even then I wouldn't have anything to do with him."

Desi felt sorry for Brian. For his mom and for his dead uncle too. "I'm sure they took good care of him at the hospice."

"It's not the same as being with your family. And now that he's dead, he'll never know how sorry I am that I treated him the way I did."

Brian buried his face in his hands. Desi wasn't sure she could handle any more sadness; she'd had enough to last her a lifetime. "You can't hate yourself forever."

"I know. But even after all this time, I'm still angry with him for getting sick."

"You never acted angry toward Alicia."

"Because Alicia never had a choice. My uncle did. He knew the risk he was taking, but he took it anyway." He stared down at his hands, stained blue by the light from the window.

"The way Alicia's mother had a choice about using drugs. I know what you mean." Desi nodded solemnly. What she also knew, but didn't say aloud, was that Alicia's mother also had a choice about having sex. Everyone did. But Desi saw clearly that sex

had consequences—especially for those too imma-
ture to handle the responsibility. Suddenly she understood that mature love, marriage, and having
babies was truly a logical progression, a natural order that got all out of whack when people jumped
into a sexual relationship outside of the framework.
For Alicia's mother the leap into sex and drugs
meant forever changing the course of her own life, as
well as saddling an innocent baby with a terrible
burden. It wasn't fair. It wasn't right.

Desi gave Brian a sideways glance, understanding his anguish over his uncle and the choices the
man had made. "Sadie said that sometimes when
you do something, you don't necessarily think about
its hurting someone else. You're only thinking about
yourself and what *you* want."

Brian heaved a sigh and hooked his elbows over
the top of the pew. "When I heard about Alicia's
being in the hospital, I felt that I had to tell you
about my uncle. I felt I owed it to you. I've never
told any of my friends." He paused. "Anyway, if you
want to tackle the project for extra credit—"

"It doesn't matter to me. We'll pass biology, no
matter what."

"That's all I wanted to do anyway," Brian admitted. "But you—well, you're smart, and I
shouldn't hold you back. You deserve an A." He
reached out and tucked some of her hair behind one
ear. His touch caused goose bumps to shiver up her
arm. "Tell me what to do to help."

"I can't think about it today. Maybe later."

He stood and pulled her up. "Fair enough, but when you are ready to think about it, let me know. If it's okay, I'd like to call and keep checking on Alicia." His kindness reached down into her heart, and she felt a gratitude she couldn't express. "Look, I know you want to get back upstairs."

"Alicia seems less agitated whenever I'm allowed to be with her," she replied. "They only let me into ICU for five minutes every hour."

"I guess you really are like a mother to her."

They parted at the elevator door. When Desi arrived back in the ICU waiting area, she discovered Gayle pacing the floor. "Alicia's taken a turn for the worse," Gayle said, her voice quivering. "It's just a matter of time before we lose her."

Chapter Seventeen

∼❧∼

Alicia was transferred to a sterile, plastic isolette. The hard protective shell contained a pair of rubber gloves that hung to the inside of the unit, and whenever Alicia needed attending, nurses placed their hands inside the gloves and took care of her. "She must be safeguarded against all germs," Aunt Clare told Desi.

Alicia looked frailer and thinner with each day. Her once round cheeks became wasted, her rib cage jutted outward, and her arms and legs erupted with sores and lesions. She wore only a diaper and was wired with a maze of tubes hooked to machines that stood in a circle around her isolette. "Can I touch her?" Desi asked.

"Only with the gloves."

Desi slipped her hands inside the unit and cupped Alicia's small head in her hand. The infant barely moved. Desi hated touching Alicia this way. The rubber acted as a barrier. "Why doesn't she look at me? Doesn't she know I'm here?"

"She's in a semicoma state," Aunt Clare explained. "But I think she knows you're here."

Desi felt a tear trickle down her cheek, but

didn't want to pull her hand out of the glove to wipe it away. "She's too little to be so sick. Does she hurt?"

"She's on pain medications."

"I've read about new drugs—experimental ones. Are the doctors trying them on Alicia? They should," Desi insisted.

"Everything possible is being done for her. Nothing can cure AIDS yet, Desi."

There *had* to be more the doctors could do. "And the coma . . . will she come out of it?"

"They don't know. Life is very tenacious, Desi. It holds on and hates to let go."

"But it *will* let go, won't it?" Desi stroked the baby's body tenderly. "I love her so much. We clicked the moment we met. Being with Alicia has meant everything. She's always had a smile for me. She's always wanted *me* to hold her."

"It's no secret that the two of you have had something unique and special."

"Maybe I've been wrong to care about her so much." Desi's voice fell to an anguished whisper. "Maybe if I didn't care so much, this wouldn't hurt so bad."

"Of course you haven't been wrong. Love takes risks, Desi, even against impossible odds. That's what *real* love is all about." Aunt Clare slipped her arm around Desi's shoulders and guided her toward the door. "Come on, honey."

Tamara was waiting in the hallway when Desi

stepped out of the ICU. They fell into each others arms. "Why is this happening to Alicia?" Desi sobbed. "She's never hurt anybody. It isn't fair."

"No, it isn't," Tamara replied in a shaky voice. "I've asked Daddy the same thing, and he says that sometimes there are no answers, that sometimes we have to leave things to heaven and just believe that someone bigger and smarter than us has life under control. The only thing we can do is love each other and be there for each other through the parts we don't understand."

Desi longed to believe that Alicia's cruel death could make sense, but she could not. Until now Desi had led an ordinary, uneventful life. Without Alicia how could she go back to it? Yet as long as Alicia was alive, Desi knew she couldn't leave her. As long as the baby hung on, there was hope. Desi clung to her dream of a miracle as a lifeline.

That evening Aunt Clare drove her home. "I want to come live with you until this is over," Desi told her when the car rolled into her driveway.

"But why?"

"Because all Mom and I do is fight about the time I spend at the hospital. She drove me once to visit Alicia, and I thought she might be coming around, but the sicker Alicia gets, the more uptight Mom becomes."

"I can't believe—"

"Believe it," Desi insisted. "The other morning

she and Dad argued about it too. She thinks it's unhealthy for me to be hanging around a dying baby. Why is she so insensitive?"

"I'm sure she doesn't mean to be."

"She hates me, Aunt Clare. She's always hated me. I'm not like Valerie, and she doesn't want anything to do with me and the things I care about."

"Oh, honey—"

Desi didn't wait for her to finish. She jumped out of the car and hurried into the house. Her mother was sitting in the living room watching TV. She looked up as Desi sped past and took the stairs two at a time. Alone in her bedroom Desi paced like a caged animal. If she could have her way about it, she'd move into the hospital. Of course that was impossible, but if she couldn't stay with her aunt, then maybe she could stay with Gayle or at the ChildCare house. There had to be some way—

She heard loud voices coming from below, her mother and her aunt arguing. Heart thudding, Desi crept down the stairs to the living room. She hung back in the shadows of the doorway, watching and listening.

"It's out of the question. Desi has a perfectly fine home right here," her mother was saying to her aunt.

"These are unusual circumstances, Eva. The girl wants to be around Alicia more. Is that too much to ask?"

"I think the whole thing's bizarre. Good heavens! Desi's not quite fifteen, and she's totally preoccupied with a sick, dying baby. It's macabre. And it's *your* fault."

"Oh really!" Aunt Clare sounded disgusted. "Desi's not some empty-headed piece of fluff, you know. She's perfectly capable of deciding for herself what she wants to do with her time."

Desi watched her mother advance toward her aunt. "How can she know? She's never tried one other thing at high school this year. It's all been that house and that baby since September."

"Listen to yourself! You're laying out her life to your standards. Maybe she *likes* working at Child-Care. Maybe she likes making her own decisions. Maybe she wants to do something meaningful with her life."

"How do you know what she wants? Or what's good for her?"

"Because I talk to her. I listen to her."

By now the sisters were practically nose to nose. "Get something straight, Clare. She's *my* daughter, not yours."

Desi saw her aunt flinch. "I know she's your daughter. You never let me forget it."

"Maybe if you weren't always poking your nose in between us, she'd be talking to me instead of you."

"Why should she?" Aunt Clare countered. "What encouragement have you ever given her?"

"You're always there to take up the slack. Always hovering in the wings, trying to take over my role."

"What a hateful thing to say. Desi needs me."

"And you're always there for her, aren't you? You're the ever present, ever attentive aunt—full of suggestions for how she should spend her free time. Why, you even have a room in your home set aside for her."

"What's that supposed to mean?"

"You've sapped Desi's and my relationship for years. Maybe if you weren't so available, she'd turn to her mother for some things." Her mother balled her fists at her side. "You can't ever make up for what happened sixteen years ago, so stop trying."

Desi saw all the color drain from her aunt's face. "So we're back to that night, are we? When are you going to forgive me—forgive yourself—for something that wasn't anybody's fault?" *What are they talking about?* Desi wondered. She heard her aunt continue, "You're not the only person in the universe to suffer a tragedy, you know, Eva. I lost someone I loved too. At least you have two daughters to fill up your life, even if you don't appreciate them the way you should." By now Aunt Clare was weeping.

Unable to take another minute of their fight, Desi hurried through the doorway. "Stop it. Stop yelling at each other." Both women whirled toward

her. Desi started to cry, even though more than anything, she wanted to be strong. "Mom, Alicia's so
sick, and I want to spend every minute with her. I
can't just disappear from her life when she needs
me. Why can't you see that?"

Tears slid down her mother's cheeks. "I just
don't want you hurt. You're still a *girl*, not a mother.
You shouldn't have to experience such an awful
thing."

"I already hurt like crazy. Please think about it,
Mom. What will hurt me the most? Alicia's dying?
Or Alicia's dying without my being with her?"

Her mother didn't answer. She stood clenching
and unclenching her fists, her face wet with tears.

Desi turned toward her aunt. "Please take me
back to the hospital, Aunt Clare. I can't stand being
in this house one more minute."

She didn't wait for her aunt to answer, but
brushed past her mother, ran outside into the frosty
night, jerked open the car door, and climbed inside.
She was so cold, her teeth chattered.

Moments later her aunt got into the car and
turned on the engine. She was crying hard. "I'll drop
you off and come back later," she told Desi.

"Can't you stay with me? I don't want to be
alone."

"I have to get myself together. I'll be back in a
while."

Desi nodded numbly, unable to sort through

what she'd heard pass between her mother and aunt. She didn't understand. All she knew was that Alicia needed her, and that she needed be with *her* baby. No one was going to stop her.

Chapter Eighteen

Desi sat staring at the cold, hard floor of the ICU waiting room. Her arms rested on her knees, and her head drooped listlessly. She was the only person around except for the night nurses. She was tired, so tired. Yet she couldn't sleep. It would be another forty-five minutes before she could get in to see Alicia. At four o'clock in the morning there wasn't anything on TV to occupy her either. There was nothing to do but sit and wait. And ache.

Desi heard someone coming down the hallway. Heels clicked hollowly against the floor. The shoes approached, but she didn't look up. They stopped in front of her. She stared down at pointed black leather toes and wondered why they looked vaguely familiar.

"Desi," her mother's voice said from above her.

Startled, Desi swung her gaze from the tips of the shoes to her mother's face. "Mom! What are you doing here?"

Her mother stood ramrod straight, holding her purse in front of her like a barrier. "I wanted to see if you were okay."

Desi averted her eyes. She was still angry at her mother. And deeply hurt.

"I thought you might like some company."

"I thought you said you found this whole thing bizarre," Desi countered.

"I said a lot of things I didn't mean to both you and my sister." Her mother's eyes were red from crying. "Can I sit with you?"

Warily Desi shifted, and her mother lowered herself to the edge of the chair beside her. "How's Alicia?"

"She's not doing well." A lump the size of a fist suddenly lodged in Desi's throat. After she mastered it, she said, "Aunt Clare will be here soon."

"No she won't. I called her and told her I'd come be with you. It's my place."

Desi jumped up. "What other mean things did you say to her?"

"Please sit down. We talked for a long time . . . straightened some things out. She agreed that I should come. I am your mother after all."

"I wish you'd never had me."

"Don't ever say that. I love you, Desi." She said the last with a catch in her voice.

Desi stared at her coolly. "You love Valerie. But me—well, not me."

Her mother released a long sigh and leaned her head back against the wall. "Clare told me that's the way you felt. I didn't believe her, but now I hear it directly from you. I need to explain some things."

"What things?"

"About how mixed up I feel inside. About how seeing you so involved with Alicia has brought back so much pain for me."

Desi's hands felt icy cold, and her feet had gone numb. She returned to her chair, but sat sideways and on the edge like a small bird poised for flight. "Alicia's dying. How can that hurt you?"

"Because—" Her mother's face contorted, and for an instant Desi thought she might lose control. "Because I keep remembering Matthew."

"My brother." Just hearing his name gave the long-ago baby form and substance. She recalled his baby book with faded ink.

"He was so beautiful, Desi, and so very, very perfect. He hardly ever cried, you know." Her mother's expression had gone soft, and her eyes glowed. "Such a good little boy too. That night, I bathed him, powdered him, dressed him in this soft green flannel sleeper. The kind with the little rubber pads on the soles of the feet."

Desi knew exactly. Alicia had a pink one. And she knew the smell of baby powder too, sweet and fresh. "What night?" she asked.

"*That* night . . ." she repeated, as if Desi had been there and could remember it. "I kissed him and put him in his crib, on his tummy, the way he liked best to sleep. Your father and I were going out to dinner and a movie. Clare was baby-sitting."

"I didn't know Aunt Clare sat for you."

"She usually did. I would never had entrusted Valerie and a new baby to some teenager." Her mother fumbled for her purse and extracted a tissue, which she wound methodically around her forefinger.

"When we came home, I checked on Val and Matthew; they were sleeping. Aunt Clare left, and your dad and I went to bed. I woke up at six the next morning. My heart was pounding, and I felt afraid. I felt that something was wrong, but I didn't know what. Then I remembered that Matthew hadn't woken up for his two A.M. feeding." Her mother's voice had grown soft, but her sentences were quick and steady, as if describing a scene from a movie.

"I ran to Matthew's room, and there he was, lying in his crib, his eyes still closed, exactly as I'd left him the night before. He wasn't moving. He wasn't breathing. I touched him, and he felt cold. I started screaming and couldn't stop." Desi's mother halted her story. Her hands were trembling, and tears were streaming down her cheeks.

"They called it crib death. The doctors couldn't tell us much about it. Only that seemingly perfectly healthy babies stopped breathing in their sleep and died. No reason. No medical explanation. No cure. Aunt Clare tells us medicine is now able to better predict babies who are vulnerable. There are monitors that keep constant vigil on their breathing. If a baby stops breathing, the monitor sounds an alarm, and a parent can administer CPR. But they didn't have those when Matthew was born."

Desi felt tortured, unable to think of a single thing to ease her mother's anguish over reliving the night Matthew died. Down the hall Alicia lay dying, so Desi understood what that part felt like. But her parents had had no warning. No dread disease. No way to prepare. "I'm sorry, Mom."

"For the longest time I believed his death was my fault."

"But it couldn't have been," Desi cried impetuously, "if no one knows what causes crib death!"

"In my mind I went over and over every detail of that night. Had I sprinkled too much powder on him, and had it clogged his lungs? Had he caught a chill from too cool bathwater?"

She knotted the tissue and stared at the shredded mess in her hands. "I even thought that maybe Aunt Clare had caused it. Maybe she'd covered him too tightly and he'd smothered."

"Oh, Mom—"

"I know," Mrs. Mitchell interrupted Desi's protest. "It wasn't rational thinking, but I couldn't help it. I just couldn't believe that my beautiful, perfect, healthy baby boy was dead and no one knew why."

Desi heard her mother take a long, shaky breath. "We survived, your father and I. We still had Valerie, and by the time she was four, I could tell she'd be a natural at tennis. I poured myself into her. She was bright and adorable, and she helped me forget." She sniffed and ran her fingers through her tangled dark hair. "Then, unexpectedly, I got pregnant again."

"I was an accident," Desi stated, affirming aloud what she'd already secretly known—she hadn't been wanted. Like Alicia.

"You were unplanned, not unwanted, Desi. But I didn't know how to relate to you. Something was wrong inside my heart. The whole time I carried you, I felt detached from the pregnancy, as if I were a surrogate of some sort. As if I were carrying you for some other woman. I know that's hard to understand."

Desi wanted to tell her that it was easy to understand. Hadn't she felt as if Alicia were hers? Willed and gifted to her by a world unable to deal with an infant with a deadly disease? Her mother continued. "After you were born, I was terrified of you—*for* you. I could barely stand to put you to bed each night. I was so afraid that you might die too. I guess I figured that if I didn't get attached, then it wouldn't hurt so bad if you left, the way Matthew did."

"I used to think there was something wrong with me. That I wasn't special like Valerie."

"It wasn't you—it was *me.* All I can tell you is that it was easier to care for you if I detached myself from you. Val was a big help when you were a baby, you know. She'd play with you for hours, read to you, feed you cookies. Then as you got older and you didn't need so much attention . . ." She shrugged.

Desi accepted what hadn't been spoken—over time she learned to get along in the family without much attention. "Val told me she remembered how she and Aunt Clare took me for walks. What about Daddy?"

"He retreated into his work. In many ways he never comes home from his job. But he has always been very proud of you, Desi, and of your science smarts. He really hopes you'll decide to become a doctor."

"I hope I get to be a doctor too," she said. "Maybe I can help babies like Matthew and Alicia." Hearing her mother's explanation helped Desi immensely. It didn't make her hurt go away, but it made it more bearable. She turned her attention toward the closed door of ICU. "Alicia's changed my life. It hurt me that you didn't understand. Didn't seem to care."

"Oh, Desi, I understood, too well. I know what it feels like to bury a baby you love. After Matthew died, I wrote a poem for him. We put part of it on his headstone." She shut her eyes and recited, " 'If all our fondest memories could be kept and never spent, We'd treasure most this chip of time, Where Matthew came and went.' "

Desi's mother stopped talking, and in the silence Desi heard the mechanical drone of the air-conditioning system and down the hall, a door closing. She wished she were older, wiser, had something to say that might erase the years of loss for them both. But nothing came to mind, so she simply stood and whispered, "I'm sorry about your baby, Mom."

Her mother looked her in the eye. "And I'm sorry about yours."

"I need to go see her." Desi checked the clock. "They'll let me in now."

"Can I go in with you?"

"You'd do that?"

"Yes. I want to see this baby you love so much."

Her mother took her hand, and they went in together. Nothing in the room had changed; nothing there announced that it was almost five A.M. and the world would soon be waking. Within the bubble Alicia's tiny chest rose and fell with the aid of the respirator. Tubes snaked from her mouth and nose. IV lines were hooked to her foot. Very carefully Desi slipped her hands inside the rubber gloves and touched the frail body.

As if the baby sensed Desi's presence, a shiver ran along her body. "I'm here, Alicia," Desi whispered. "Right here."

"Dear God," Desi heard her mother say. "Oh, Desi. It's breaking my heart."

Hearing the emotion in her mother's voice, Desi glanced over her shoulder. "You can touch her through the gloves if you want. They say it's good for the dying to be touched." Desi withdrew her hands and stepped aside.

Slowly, with hesitation, her mother inched forward. Copying Desi's motions, she slid her hands into the gloves protruding inside the plastic bubble. She maneuvered them awkwardly, but eventually was able to pat Alicia's back. Another tremor shook the little body. "It's so unfair," her mother whispered. "Unfair that babies die before they've ever had a chance to live."

Desi had the eerie feeling that although her mother was touching Alicia, she was seeing Matthew. For a single moment she saw him too, lying on his tummy the way her mother had described, smelling of powder and looking so warm and soft in his green flannel sleeper. An unbearable aching filled her, coupled with a longing to hold the brother she never knew. She trembled, fought against tears that dammed behind her eyes. "We have to go, Mom," she said. "They only allow visitors a few minutes."

Slowly Desi's mother removed her hands from the gloves, and even more slowly stepped backward. Finally she turned and walked quickly to the door. Before following, Desi allowed herself one long, lingering look at Alicia. At the crystal bubble that surrounded her. At the tubes and fluids and machines that supported her. At the chip of time that held her captive. Like a sparrow waiting to be set free.

Chapter Nineteen

Three nights later Gayle called for Desi to come immediately to the hospital. Desi yelled for her mother, paused only long enough to grab her coat and a small paper sack, and ran for the car. Her mother drove like a mad person to the hospital, where they abandoned the car at the emergency room parking lot entrance and raced inside. Frantically Desi pushed past other visitors and ran up the stairwell to the pediatric floor. She arrived so winded that she felt lightheaded.

She saw Gayle and her aunt standing outside the door of ICU. "The pneumonia's taken over. Her respiration's doubled, and her heartbeat's over two hundred—her heart is literally beating itself to death," Gayle told her.

"I want to be with her."

"When the doctor comes out."

Desi tugged on the sterile gloves that her aunt handed her, while down the hall the elevator doors opened and her mother hurried along the corridor toward them. "How is she?" Desi's mom asked breathlessly.

"We're losing her," Aunt Clare replied.

Desi felt as if daggers had been jammed into her heart.

The door to isolation swung open, the doctor emerged, and his eyes told Desi everything. She braced herself against the wall and heard him say, "She's gone."

Stunned by the finality of his words, Desi felt as if the walls were closing in on her. She held back her tears and asked, "Can I be with her? For one last time?"

Aunt Clare glanced at Desi's mother, who nodded. "Give me a minute," Aunt Clare said, starting into the room.

"Wait." Desi took her arm. "Take this for her."

Her aunt took the paper bag and minutes later held the door ajar for Desi, saying, "Just for a quick good-bye." She stepped outside so that Desi could be alone.

An eerie silence blanketed the room. The monitors had been turned off, their screens vacant, their sentry duty over. The isolette was open, like a broken eggshell. Within, Alicia lay on the white sheeting—still, so very, very still. The tubes and IV lines had been pulled, and Aunt Clare had dressed Alicia in the beautiful red velvet dress Desi had bought her for Christmas.

Alicia's eyes were closed, and she looked as if she were asleep. Desi stood beside the ruptured bubble and traced the infant's perfect features with her eyes—lashes, mouth, button nose.

She tugged off the latex gloves and dropped them onto the floor. Gently Desi lifted up the baby. Alicia's body felt feather light, and she smelled of her medications. The baby's small arms hung limply, and her fingers were already stiffening. But her skin was still warm, and as long as she felt warm, Desi couldn't let her go.

The valley of the shadow of death. Desi knew what a valley was, and now, for the first time, she understood what the shadow of death looked like. Alicia's skin had taken on a dusty, gray hue. No flow of blood to turn her skin its usual dark, glowing sepia. No flutter of breath from her lungs. Life had fled, and with it, the soft, sweet scent of hope.

She rocked Alicia, cooing softly, whispered her name and reminded her of her yellow bath duck, her stuffed animals, her favorite blanket. She wondered if God would allow her to have such things in heaven.

Aunt Clare came in. "We have to go, honey."

"It's hard to leave her."

"I know."

Desi tenderly placed Alicia back inside the fractured isolette, smoothed her dress, and twirled a soft black ringlet of hair around her finger.

"She looks beautiful," Aunt Clare said. "Like an angel."

Desi bent over and ever so gently rubbed her

nose on Alicia's and whispered, "Good-bye, baby girl."

The corridor was empty when Desi stepped outside Alicia's room. Gayle had gone to fill out paperwork, and the nurses were busy with night rounds. She found her mother in the small room where they'd met and talked nights before. She was looking out on the glittering Atlanta skyline when Desi came in with her aunt. She turned, and when their gazes met, Desi felt the tears she'd so carefully held inside start flowing.

She began to shake, her teeth chattering, and a burning, aching sensation clogged her throat. "Alicia's dead, Mom," was all she could manage before her voice broke.

Beside her she heard her aunt say, "Desi, sit down, honey. Come on, let me get you something."

Eva Mitchell stepped forward. "I'll take her now, Clare," Desi's mother said. "I've been down this road before." She held her arms open, and Desi fell into them, sobbing. "I'm sorry, Desi . . . very, very sorry. I know you loved her. And I know how it feels."

Desi realized that her mother *did* know, because she had lost a baby too. She clung to her mother so tightly that her arms ached. Her mother held her, rocked her, smoothed her hair. At some point Desi reached out toward her aunt, and the three of them stood in a circle and wept as one.

* * *

The staff and volunteers of ChildCare held a small memorial service for Alicia on the property of the facility. The January day had broken bitter cold, and even though the sun was shining, Desi couldn't feel its warmth. Her mother accompanied her, and they listened as Reverend Wilcox presented a verbal picture of Alicia in a far, far better place, where there was no more pain and suffering and where every tear would be wiped away.

Desi looked to the barren trees, remembering when they'd been bright with autumn colors and she'd walked Alicia along the winding pathways. Now the trees looked dead, empty and stripped. Her heart felt hollow. As barren and hard as the red Georgia clay beneath her feet.

After the brief ceremony people hugged her— Gayle, Sadie, Tamara, Aunt Clare. The reporter who'd interviewed her at Christmas was there too. "I'm doing another story to help publicize the plight of these babies and stress the needs of ChildCare. I can't begin to tell you the response we got at the paper over the first story. The mail was tremendous. People were impressed by you and Tamara, that you volunteered so much of your time when you could have been doing other things."

The reporter studied Desi thoughtfully. "I know Alicia had special significance to you. Can I tell our readers what you're experiencing?"

Desi stared blankly, not certain how to answer. How did she put the intensity of her pain into words? "I'll miss her," was about all she could think to say.

"This has been hard on my daughter," her mother interjected, putting her arm around Desi protectively. "She loved that little girl."

The reporter turned to her. "You must be very proud of Desi."

"I am."

Gayle came over and invited them all inside out of the cold. "I'd like to show you around, Mrs. Mitchell. The babies are napping now, and you can see our home and where Desi's worked all these months."

Desi motioned for them to go on because she knew that she couldn't go back inside. She couldn't stand to see the rooms, the furniture, the place where Alicia once lived and laughed. "I'd like to be alone for a while," she told her mother.

"Are you certain?"

"I feel like walking around the grounds."

"I won't be long," her mother assured her.

Desi watched her mother enter the house, then strolled aimlessly to the outer edges of the property, where the brick wall rose to block off the street. She kicked at a clump of earth and tried to think about what she knew she had to do. She had to go back to school and finish the term. She had to think about English and biology and math and . . . A tear slid down her cheek. How could she?

"Are you Desi?" The soft accented voice came

from behind her. Startled, she spun, and her eyes opened wide in recognition. "They say you're the one who stuck with my baby till the end." The young girl tipped her head shyly. "I'm Sherrie. I was Alicia's mama."

"I didn't see you at the service."

"I was there." Her large, dark eyes seemed to fill her small face. "I saw my baby at the funeral home before they closed up her coffin and took her away. That was a fine dress you picked out for her. She looked real pretty. Like a baby doll."

Unsure of how to respond, Desi only nodded. Sherrie continued. "I don't want you to be thinking I was a bad mama. I loved my little girl. I couldn't take care of her 'cause I was sick for a long time. I'm not using drugs no more, and the doctors . . . well . . . they got me taking AZT and other medicine to keep my sickness in control."

With a sinking feeling, Desi realized that Sherrie was as infected with HIV as Alicia had been. As Brian's uncle had been. The fact that the girl had cleaned up her life wasn't going to take away the terrible illness that faced her. Desi swallowed hard and mumbled, "I'm glad for you."

"I don't want you thinking that I meant to give my baby AIDS either."

"I never figured you did."

The wind blew Sherrie's short hair, and she reached up and poked it behind her ear. "I've been getting myself back together. I'm going back to high school this summer." She held her head high, as if proud of her choice.

Desi recalled all the venomous thoughts she'd held toward Sherrie. She remembered spying on her and Alicia in the park, and she remembered how afraid she'd been that Sherrie would reclaim her daughter. Now, looking at the slender teen, her smooth, brown skin, her plain clothing and unaffected expression, Desi felt no more animosity toward her. As Desi considered Sherrie's future and the possibilities that it held, she felt respect for the girl. Choosing to do something worthwhile for herself instead of dropping back into her old lifestyle took courage. "I hope you get your diploma," she told Sherrie.

"I was going to take my baby back and raise her up and give her a good home. When the social worker called me and said my baby was in the hospital dying . . ." Sherrie hugged her arms to her chest and turned her eyes heavenward. "I got to see her once before she got sick. I got to hold her when the social worker brought her to me for a visit. It was at a nice park." For a moment Sherrie looked thoughtful. "I'll bet you dressed her to come see me that time, didn't you?"

Mutely Desi nodded.

"Anyway that's how I wanted to remember her. All pretty like she was at the funeral home. Not sick like I knew she'd be in the hospital. You know what I'm saying, don't you?"

Desi assured Sherrie she understood. She said, "I really cared about Alicia. She was special."

"Yes, she *was* special, wasn't she?"

Desi heard her mother call to her from the driveway and told Sherrie, "I have to go."

"Well, I'm glad I got to say thank you for helping Alicia. Thank you for taking care of her when I couldn't."

Desi told Sherrie good-bye and hurried over to her mother. "I want to go home."

"Are you all right?"

Her teeth chattered. "I'm cold."

In the car her mother turned up the heater. "I'm impressed with the facility, Desi. It's amazing what they've done strictly through donations. Gayle seems very competent. She told me how much she likes you and how pleased she is to have you working there."

Desi stared out the window. Her mother gave her a sideways glance. "I know I argued against your working there. I should have been more understanding. I won't bother you anymore about your volunteer work at ChildCare."

"Don't worry, Mom. I'm through with it."

"Through?"

"Now that Alicia's gone, I don't want to go back. I know there are other babies who need to be cared for, but it's over for me."

"I see." They rode in silence until her mother broke it. "You may change your mind."

"No. I can't go back." Tears brimmed in her eyes, and the scenery became a blur. She held her hands in front of the heater. The warm air flowed over them, but still she shivered. Alicia was gone, and so was Desi's desire to be a part of charity work. It was a fact—babies with AIDS died. There was no need for her to think anything she could do could ever make a difference. No need at all.

Chapter Twenty

～⌒ঌ～

The hot May sun beat down on Desi's head and shoulders. From her seat in the grandstand she could see the tennis court perfectly. Valerie volleyed a ball over the net, and Desi nervously reached for her mother's hand and squeezed it. One more point, and Val would win. She heard the thwack of the yellow ball on the racket, watched it clear the net, saw Val's opponent return it, and then saw Val deliver a wicked forehand that slammed the ball to the backside of the court far out of her opponent's reach. "Set point!" the announcer declared. The crowd stood and cheered.

Seeing Val win gave Desi enormous satisfaction. It meant that the University of Florida would advance to the collegiate regional championships and that Val, top seeded on her team, would be nationally ranked. Later in the locker room area, their mother exclaimed, "We're so proud of you!" She gave Val a hug.

Val grinned, thrust her winner's bouquet of roses into Desi's arms, and said, "Thanks, Mom. For everything."

"You've worked hard. You deserve it," their

mom insisted. She glanced down at her watch. "You and Desi visit one another while I go rescue your coach from your father. He was asking him a million questions about this summer. We're both so pleased that you've been asked to attend the Olympic training camp. What an honor."

Val hugged her mother and waved as she walked away.

"You're going to the Olympic training camp?" Desi asked.

"You bet," Val cried, pulling the rubber band from her hair and digging in her duffel bag for her brush. All around them other girls were hurriedly changing and freshening up for the long drive back to the campus.

"So I guess you feel better than you did at Thanksgiving and Christmas."

"Absolutely! But I think a lot of it's because Mom's stopped pressuring me to be perfect at tennis and my studies." Val fluffed her long black hair and dug for a barrette. "Letting me drop a course so that I could concentrate on tennis also helped. I honestly couldn't handle both." Val paused thoughtfully. "She and Dad seem to be hitting it off better too. And you two are less uptight around each other. What gives?"

"She's been trying harder lately."

"I was surprised when she wrote that she'd dropped back to part-time work again. Do you know why?"

"She told me that she felt it was about time she

and I got to know each other better. We've been spending more time together."

Val wrinkled her nose. "I hope she's not cramping your life. I mean you *are* in high school, with better things to do than hang around with your mother."

Desi honestly didn't mind. How could Val understand that for Desi her mother's attention was a welcome change? Ever since the night of Alicia's death there had been a bond between them, a cord of understanding and mutual respect. "It's not so bad," she told her sister. "I'm not doing much of anything else now anyway."

"You've never gone back to ChildCare?"

Desi averted her eyes and shook her head. "I couldn't go back after Alicia died. I'm just concentrating on school. I'm not sure what I'll be doing when it's out for the summer."

"Is it smart to never go back?" Val asked, hastily adding, "I know what it's like to be pounded by an opponent. It makes me want to give up tennis forever, but I know I'd be worse off if I just quit altogether."

Desi realized what Val was telling her. Aunt Clare had said much the same thing when Desi told her of her decision to quit her volunteer work at ChildCare. Aunt Clare had pleaded, "Don't give up, Desi. There are babies there who need you and who will remember you if you come back."

"All that job did was make me hurt," Desi had

insisted, struggling with the burden of guilt she felt over leaving. "It caused all sorts of trouble at home, at school, between you and Mom."

"Ever since that night"—Aunt Clare hadn't said "since Alicia died," but Desi knew what night she meant—"Eva and I have worked out a lot of our differences. The argument was hard, but in the long run it served a good purpose. We've both been able to talk about the night Matthew died. Before now she never would." Aunt Clare touched Desi's arm. "You aren't responsible for our relationship. We are. Don't let anything keep you from coming back to ChildCare if you want to."

"I don't want to," Desi said stonily. "I can't."

Now, in the empty locker room with Val, Desi gazed down at the fragrant bouquet of roses cradled in her arms. Even months later she still found it difficult to talk about the infant. "I miss Alicia." The green paper wrapped around the roses rustled. "The last week or so that she lived was really hard to get through."

"I can only imagine." Val snapped the barrette in place. "I guess it was good that Mom came around at the end and went with you to the hospital. I don't know how you stood it, watching that poor, sweet baby die."

"Mom helped me a lot," Desi replied, absently running her fingers over the deep red petals. "She understood more than I ever thought." Desi didn't add that they'd had many conversations about her mother's loss of Matthew. It was as if a gate had opened in her mother's heart and allowed her pent-up memories and feelings to pour through.

"I'm glad things are working out for you," Val said. She zipped up her bag. "How's that cute guy—Brian?"

"I told you—we're just lab partners." In truth Desi didn't have much more to tell. Except for the extra time they'd put in on their science fair project, Desi had had little to do with Brian. It wasn't that she didn't want to be with him. She did. But she needed time for her heart to stop hurting.

"Well, I still think he's cute, so don't blow it." Val stood and looked around to see that she'd gathered all her belongings. "When will you know if your project makes it to the state finals?"

"Another week."

"I hope you go all the way."

"Well, it's not like winning regionals in collegiate tennis," Desi told Val with a hint of teasing. "I'll miss you when you go off to camp this summer," she added.

"Oh, I'll be home for a whole month before camp starts. Now that Mom's taken the pressure off, I'm actually looking forward to it."

One of the girls from the tennis team poked her head through the doorway and yelled, "Hey, Mitchell! The coach is holding the van. Get a move on it."

"Coming!" Val picked up her bag and racket. "Listen, I'm glad you came to watch me play."

"I wouldn't have missed it. You're my favorite sister. Don't you want to take your roses with you?" Desi asked as Val darted out the door.

"You're my *only* sister. Take them home and enjoy them," Val called over her shoulder. "Let's hope there's plenty more in my future at regionals."

Desi sniffed the heady sweetness of the red bouquet as she followed her sister into the sunlight.

A week later Desi decided it was past time to throw the red roses out. The petals had grown dark with age, and the aroma had turned stale. She was walking them to the trash can when she passed the den and saw her mother sitting on the floor surrounded by photos, papers, and books. Intrigued, Desi stepped into the room. "What're you doing?"

Her mother glanced up, and Desi saw a mist of tears in her blue eyes. "Are you okay, Mom?"

Her mother quickly wiped the back of her hand over her eyes. "I'm fine."

"You're crying."

"Not really. Just reminiscing."

Setting the flowers down on the carpet, Desi knelt beside her mother and saw that she was holding a silver-framed photograph of a newborn baby. "Matthew?"

"Yes. They took it at the hospital right after he was born." Her mother held the frame up for Desi to see.

The baby's brow was puckered, his eyes were narrow slits. A fine cap of dark hair covered his egg-shaped head, and his fists were curled tightly beside plump cheeks. "Gee, he looks like a little old man."

Her mother laughed softly. "Newborns usually aren't beautiful to anybody but their parents."

"I guess they cuten up as they get older, huh?"

"They certainly do." Her mother held up a snapshot of herself holding a slightly older version of the baby. He was dressed in blue and wrapped in a blue blanket. "He's two months old here." She held up another. "And three months here."

Twin dimples peeked out from either side of his fat, rosy cheeks. "You still miss him, don't you?"

"I'll always miss him." Her mother picked up a tiny beaded bracelet that bore his name and fingered the beads like a rosary. "I've thought about him more these past few months than in all the years since he died. I've been realizing how much I missed with you as a baby."

"Me?"

"You were an adorable baby too." Her mother sorted through the pictures until she found one of a baby girl dressed in pink with a pink bow taped to her head.

"I never saw these before. I didn't know you had them." Desi noticed her dimples and realized that they were like Matthew's.

"We have many photos of you. I just never

showed them off. I wish I could go back and do some things differently."

"I guess everybody wishes they could do some things over again."

Her mother touched her arm. "Don't you make the same mistake."

"What do you mean?"

Her mother didn't say anything for a minute, but only stared down at the framed photo of Matthew. "Don't waste your whole life mourning what can't be changed. Don't lose sight of what's really important."

Desi knew what she was telling her. She wanted her to remember Alicia, but not to get too caught up in the loss of her. But the wounds on her heart still ached, even after five months. "I know what's important," she said quickly. "I'm almost a sophomore, remember? Haven't you always told me there's plenty for me to do in high school? Maybe I'll try some new things out next year."

"That will be good for you, but don't give up all your other interests."

Desi didn't want to think about the future at the moment. She was still finding it hard to let go of the past. She watched her mother begin to sort through her baby pictures. "What are you going to do with them?"

"I going to put them in your baby book. I was glancing through it and saw that I'd hardly written down a thing. I want to go back and fix it up while I can still remember your milestones." She smiled. "Someday when you have children of your own, you may want to prove to them how special and brilliant you were."

Desi felt surprise, then pleasure. And she felt as if she mattered, really mattered. "Corrine's coming by, and we're going to the mall. I'd better finish getting ready." She scrambled to her feet, retrieving the limp bouquet. "And throw these away."

Desi was almost out the door when her mother added, "By the way, congratulations again on your science fair project's being passed on to the state level. In case I didn't tell you when you first showed it to me, I found it very touching that you chose to do something on sudden infant death syndrome."

"Brian helped a lot," Desi said, remembering how he'd come through for her when she'd suggested the topic and explained about her baby brother. "Plus I had a whole lot more time to work on it than I ever thought I would."

Desi hurried to the kitchen, where she stepped on the pedal to open the trash can. The lid popped up, but she stood staring down at the half-dead flowers, suddenly unable to dump them. Every petal was edged in brown. Several fell off in her hand, and she fingered them. They felt soft, reminding her of velvet. Their aroma clung to her skin. She shook the stems, and petals fluttered downward, then lay scattered on the cool white tile, like scales.

Chapter Twenty-one

❧

June's sultry heat soaked through Desi's cotton shirt as she walked slowly along the driveway of the ChildCare house. She switched the cardboard box she was carrying to her other hip, and squinted into the distance where someone was steering a riding lawn mower around the trees and bushes on the property.

Suddenly the lawn tractor turned and headed her way. The roar of the engine split the air, and the smell of gas exhaust blotted out the scents of honeysuckle and mown grass. When it was almost on top of her, Brian, the driver, cut the engine and hopped off. "Desi? I thought that was you!" His tan made his hair seem blonder and his eyes bluer. "How are you doing? Why are you here?"

"I could ask the same thing," she said, unable to hide her surprise at seeing him. "I thought you were working at the health club this summer."

"I am. But I volunteer here two weekends a month, doing yard work. They sure need the help." He wiped sweat from his forehead. "So what have you been doing since school let out?"

"I've been filling in for my dad's receptionist

while she's on vacation—answering phones and setting up appointments." She looked around the expansive yard. The bushes were clipped, and mulch had been spread around the bases of hedges and trees. "The place looks nice. Better than before."

"Yeah, well, I wanted to help out, and I knew I'd be no good juggling babies—the way they poop and all."

He made a face, and she smiled. "I got an A in biology," she said. "Did you?"

"Sure did, but I've created a monster. My report card had mostly C's, a D-plus, and one glowing A. My mom keeps calling me 'my son, the doctor.'"

They stood looking at each other in the hot, sticky air until Brian said, "You told me you'd quit after Alicia died. I didn't think you'd come back."

Desi swatted at a fly that buzzed around her hair. "I didn't plan to. I didn't think I could stand coming here and not seeing her. Even now it's hard to think about the babies inside and how they could get sick and die."

"Gayle told me that Dwayne had his first birthday and that his most recent results showed he's not testing HIV-positive anymore. They think he'll be all right, it's possible that he may never develop AIDS."

"I'm glad."

Brian pointed to the box she carried. "So what you got there? Some kind of plant?"

She adjusted her grip on the box. "Believe it or

not, it's a rosebush. I thought I'd plant it under the nursery window."

"I can do it for you."

She pulled back. "No. Uh—thanks, but I want to do it." She felt she owed him an explanation. "It's a dumb idea I had. I know it looks like a naked stick with its bottom wrapped in burlap, but the guy at the nursery where I bought it swears that it'll be blooming in no time. It's supposed to have giant, red velvet roses with some fancy name that I can't remember. The man said it'll need plenty of water."

"Would you like me to take care of it?"

"Could you?" She appreciated his offer, knowing she'd failed to consider its upkeep once it was planted.

"No problem." He looked around. "Well, I'd better get back to work."

"And I'd better get this thing in the ground. It was good to see you again."

"Yeah. You too." He climbed back onto the riding mower, but paused before switching on the engine. "I was wondering if maybe sometime this summer you'd like to go to a movie with me."

Her heart thumped, and she felt a funny fluttering sensation inside her tummy. "A movie?"

"Nothing with blood and guts," he warned with a grin.

"Sure. I'd like to a lot."

"I'll call you." He waved and started the motor. The engine roared as he zigzagged in and out of the trees. Soon the sound of the motor was replaced by the humming of insects, and the smell of gasoline displaced by the sweet scent of the honeysuckle. *A real date with Brian.* She grinned and looked forward to telling Corrine.

Desi boosted the box and headed for the window outside the room where Alicia once lived.

"Brian said you were out here."

Desi looked up at Gayle, hastily wiped her dirt-covered palms on her shorts, and shielded her eyes against the glare of the sun. Gayle was tan and trimmer than the last time Desi had seen her. "I'm planting a rosebush. I hope you don't mind."

"Not a bit. We're trying hard to fix the place up. Your friend Brian's been a great help."

"He really understands about AIDS and the babies and all."

"Yes, he told me about his uncle." Gayle regarded the bush skeptically. "Is it alive?"

"I know it doesn't look like much right now, but the man at the nursery promised it'd be spouting roses in a few weeks."

"Why are you planting it?"

Desi didn't answer right away, but patted the red Georgia dirt firmly around the base and stood. "I started thinking about how Alicia only lived for such a little bit of time, and how she'd never get to grow up. She'd have been pretty, don't you think?"

"She would have been beautiful."

"Well, I thought there should be something pretty to remember her by. A rosebush seemed like a good idea."

Gayle looked thoughtful. "You mean like a living memorial?"

"Something like that."

"I love it. In fact I love it a lot. We could put a memorial garden here on the grounds. Something with benches, for quiet meditation. A kind of living monument to all these babies." Gayle rubbed her hands together gleefully. "What an excellent idea. I'll bring it up at our next board meeting. Maybe we can set aside some money for it."

Desi was pleased by Gayle's enthusiasm, but she had wanted to plant something just for Alicia—and for Matthew. Still she said, "It sounds all right to me. I hope the board approves."

Gayle put her arm around Desi's shoulders. "How have you been? We've missed you. Tamara especially."

"I'm okay." A swarm of memories pressed in on Desi—walking Alicia in her stroller, bathing the babies, feeding and changing them, Christmas and the decorating party. She felt a lump rising to her throat and realized she needed to get out of there.

"Why don't you come inside and have some lemonade? Sadie's just made a fresh pitcher. She's baking cookies too."

"I've got to be going. Mom's picking me up soon."

"It's awful hot out here, and that lemonade is ice-cold."

Desi warred with her emotions. "Well, maybe for one glass."

Inside the house the air-conditioning felt cool, refreshing. She lifted her long hair off her neck and looked around. Fresh mauve paint, matched floral-patterned sofas, and gorgeous arrangements of silk flowers made the living room look like a page from a decorator's magazine. "The place looks wonderful," Desi said in genuine admiration.

"Your mother's touch," Gayle told her.

"My mother? She never said a word."

"I think she wanted to give you plenty of space about the whole thing. We all knew how you were grieving." Gayle led her into the newly furnished playroom. "Your mother's really been fantastic. She knows so many decorators and merchants. She managed to get donations of furniture and materials."

Gayle paused in front of a photo gallery of the ChildCare infants on the wall. Desi purposefully avoided looking at it, concentrating instead on the bookshelf below that held scrapbooks and various memorabilia. Her gaze snagged on the binding of the baby book she'd bought Alicia. Had anyone filled it in? She longed for the courage to check, but didn't find it.

She followed Gayle into the kitchen, where several of the volunteers sat eating lunch. "I heard you were visiting," Sadie said, embracing Desi. "It's wonderful to see you again. Can you stay? Tamara will be here soon, and she'd love to see you."

"I can't. Honest." Desi felt trapped. All she wanted to do was get out.

Sadie grabbed her hand and pulled her down the hall. "Come see the babies before you go. We've got two new ones. Of course it's nap time right now, so you'll be seeing them at their best."

"But I can't—"

Sadie ushered her into one of the bedrooms. "Shh. Just take a peek." Desi felt a tightening in her chest. She was in Alicia's old room. Muted sunlight shimmered through sheer white curtains and a partially drawn window shade. "Look at this one," Sadie urged, leaning over Alicia's old crib. Sadie lifted a tightly wound bundle off the elevated mattress. "This here is Lucas."

Reluctantly Desi peered at a tiny dark face within the folds of the blanket. His features were wizened, like an old man's, and a stocking hat covered his head.

"He was born five weeks premature and is just now topping six pounds. It was touch and go for a spell—he was born HIV-positive and cocaine-addicted—but he's scrappy. We've had him with us for two weeks."

Desi inspected Lucas and the bed, Alicia's bed. The sheets were now pale blue, the blanket sported turtles in football gear, and the stuffed animals were all brand-new. Her heart twisted. It was as if Alicia had never existed.

"Oops," Sadie said suddenly. "There goes the timer for my cookies. Here." She handed the baby over to Desi, who juggled the bundle awkwardly.

"But I don't want—"

"I'll be right back," Sadie called softly, hurrying out the door.

For a moment Desi didn't move. Air felt trapped in her lungs. She didn't want to be there. She didn't want to be holding Lucas. In her arms the baby squirmed and whimpered, reminding her of a mewing kitten. "Don't wake up," she pleaded. Lucas's eyes remained closed, and Desi let her breath out slowly. He settled down, and she started to lay him in the crib, but saw the rocker by the window and decided to rock him so that he'd stay asleep.

He weighed next to nothing in her arms. She pulled the blanket away from his face and studied him. He wasn't a very pretty baby, she decided. His nose seemed too large for his face, and his chin jutted. No, he wasn't much to look at. Maybe he'd look better when he filled out, got some weight on him. Desi sighed.

Sunlight spilled onto her lap. Outside she could see the bush she'd planted beneath the window. Rising out of the packed Georgia clay, it looked forlorn, like a stripped stick, and she shook her head in disgust. If that man at the nursery had sold her a dud

. . . Again she looked down at the baby. "I suppose I'll have to come and keep an eye on the thing," she grumbled. Yes, that's what she'd have to do. She'd have to return to carefully watch it, in order to make certain that it bloomed.

Desi hugged Lucas closer and began to rock back and forth. She knew Alicia would never see the flowers, but perhaps Lucas would. Perhaps he'd be one of the lucky ones who escaped AIDS to grow into a normal, healthy boy. Only time would tell.

Absently Desi began to hum a lullaby while Lucas slept nestled in her arms, and soft summer sunlight floated through the window and danced on his tiny face.